The young woman's colorful skirt swirled high in the air as she spun through the intricate steps of the dance, revealing lithe, muscular brown legs. She raised her arms above her head as she tossed the mane of tumbled, midnight black curls from side to side. Her full breasts bobbed, threatening to escape from the confines of the low-cut white blouse that left her sleek shoulders bare.

Longarm tapped a booted toe in time to the music coming from the twin guitars of the two brothers playing them. He enjoyed a lively tune, and he certainly appreciated the beautiful sight of the young woman as she danced.

Of course, he probably would have appreciated it a mite more if he hadn't been pretty damn sure that somebody in this cantina wanted to kill him . . .

DON'T MISS THESE
ALL-ACTION WESTERN SERIES
FROM THE BERKLEY PUBLISHING GROUP

THE GUNSMITH by J. R. Roberts
Clint Adams was a legend among lawmen, outlaws, and ladies. They called him . . . the Gunsmith.

LONGARM by Tabor Evans
The popular long-running series about Deputy U.S. Marshal Custis Long—his life, his loves, his fight for justice.

SLOCUM by Jake Logan
Today's longest-running action Western. John Slocum rides a deadly trail of hot blood and cold steel.

BUSHWHACKERS by B. J. Lanagan
An action-packed series by the creators of Longarm! The rousing adventures of the most brutal gang of cutthroats ever assembled—Quantrill's Raiders.

DIAMONDBACK by Guy Brewer
Dex Yancey is Diamondback, a Southern gentleman turned con man when his brother cheats him out of the family fortune. Ladies love him. Gamblers hate him. But nobody pulls one over on Dex . . .

WILDGUN by Jack Hanson
The blazing adventures of mountain man Will Barlow—from the creators of Longarm!

TEXAS TRACKER by Tom Calhoun
J.T. Law: the most relentless—and dangerous—manhunter in all Texas. Where sheriffs and posses fail, he's the best man to bring in the most vicious outlaws—for a price.

→ TABOR EVANS ←

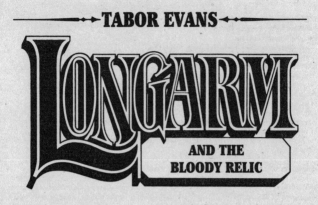

LONGARM

AND THE
BLOODY RELIC

JOVE BOOKS, NEW YORK

THE BERKLEY PUBLISHING GROUP
Published by the Penguin Group
Penguin Group (USA) Inc.
375 Hudson Street, New York, New York 10014, USA

Penguin Group (Canada), 90 Eglinton Avenue East, Suite 700, Toronto, Ontario M4P 2Y3, Canada
(a division of Pearson Penguin Canada Inc.)
Penguin Books Ltd., 80 Strand, London WC2R 0RL, England
Penguin Group Ireland, 25 St. Stephen's Green, Dublin 2, Ireland (a division of Penguin Books Ltd.)
Penguin Group (Australia), 250 Camberwell Road, Camberwell, Victoria 3124, Australia
(a division of Pearson Australia Group Pty. Ltd.)
Penguin Books India Pvt. Ltd., 11 Community Centre, Panchsheel Park, New Delhi—110 017, India
Penguin Group (NZ), 67 Apollo Drive, Rosedale, North Shore 0632, New Zealand
(a division of Pearson New Zealand Ltd.)
Penguin Books (South Africa) (Pty.) Ltd., 24 Sturdee Avenue, Rosebank, Johannesburg 2196,
South Africa

Penguin Books Ltd., Registered Offices: 80 Strand, London WC2R 0RL, England

This is a work of fiction. Names, characters, places, and incidents either are the product of the author's imagination or are used fictitiously, and any resemblance to actual persons, living or dead, business establishments, events, or locales is entirely coincidental.

LONGARM AND THE BLOODY RELIC

A Jove Book / published by arrangement with the author

PRINTING HISTORY
Jove edition / May 2011

Copyright © 2011 by Penguin Group (USA) Inc.
Cover illustration by Milo Sinovcic.

All rights reserved.
No part of this book may be reproduced, scanned, or distributed in any printed or electronic form without permission. Please do not participate in or encourage piracy of copyrighted materials in violation of the author's rights. Purchase only authorized editions.
For information, address: The Berkley Publishing Group,
a division of Penguin Group (USA) Inc.,
375 Hudson Street, New York, New York 10014.

ISBN: 978-0-515-14936-4

JOVE®
Jove Books are published by The Berkley Publishing Group,
a division of Penguin Group (USA) Inc.,
375 Hudson Street, New York, New York 10014.
JOVE® is a registered trademark of Penguin Group (USA) Inc.
The "J" design is a trademark of Penguin Group (USA) Inc.

PRINTED IN THE UNITED STATES OF AMERICA

10 9 8 7 6 5 4 3 2 1

If you purchased this book without a cover, you should be aware that this book is stolen property. It was reported as "unsold and destroyed" to the publisher, and neither the author nor the publisher has received any payment for this "stripped book."

Chapter 1

The young woman's colorful skirt swirled high in the air as she spun through the intricate steps of the dance, revealing lithe, muscular brown legs. She raised her arms above her head as she tossed the mane of tumbled, midnight black curls from side to side. Her full breasts bobbed, threatening to escape from the confines of the low-cut white blouse that left her sleek shoulders bare.

Longarm tapped a booted toe in time to the music coming from the twin guitars of the two brothers playing them. He enjoyed a lively tune, and he certainly appreciated the beautiful sight of the young woman as she danced.

Of course, he probably would have appreciated it a mite more if he hadn't been pretty damn sure that somebody in this cantina wanted to kill him.

The guitar players finished the song with a flourish, and the dancer wound up taking a bow, which put her rounded bosom in even more danger of falling out of her blouse. As she straightened, Longarm saw that she was breathless from her exertions. The fine sheen of sweat on her forehead reflected the light from the candles stuck in wine bottles on several of the tables.

She turned, smiling, and her gaze lingered on the tall man in the tweed suit and flat-crowned, snuff brown Stetson.

Longarm's cheroot was tilted at a jaunty angle as he clamped it between his teeth and joined in the applause.

The dancer leaned over to the musicians, who looked almost as much alike as their guitars did, and spoke to them.

Then she started toward the table where Longarm sat.

He wasn't sure it was a good idea for her to join him. For one thing, he was working, so he probably didn't need the distraction a beautiful gal always provided.

For another, it might be dangerous for her. Not twenty minutes earlier, bullets had been whipping past Longarm's head as he ran through the streets of San Antonio. Trouble had a habit of following him.

But the girl sat down anyway, and he didn't tell her to go away.

"*Hola*, señor," she greeted him. "You enjoyed my dance?"

"I sure did, darlin'," Longarm said as he took the cheroot out of his mouth.

"My name is Mercedes."

"Pleased to meet you. They call me Custis."

That was only one of the things they called him. Some preferred Longarm, some addressed him as Deputy Marshal Long. And some just called him a no-good son of a bitch, usually a lawbreaking varmint he had either just arrested or shot.

Mercedes leaned forward, giving him a good look at her breasts. "Custis, if you would like for me to dance for you alone, it can be arranged. I have a place not far from here . . ."

"Is that all right with your brothers?" He had noted the family resemblance between Mercedes and the two guitar players.

She gave a defiant toss of her head. "My brothers do not tell me what to do."

"I just don't want anybody gettin' mad and tryin' to slip a knife betwixt my ribs."

"Do not worry," Mercedes said. "Eduardo and Jaime know better than to interfere with my life."

Something flashed in her eyes as she said that, and Longarm was willing to bet that she had told her brothers to butt out on more than one occasion in the past.

As tempting as it was, he knew that if he left here with her, he would be putting her life at risk, and he was too much of a gentleman to do that.

He opened his mouth to tender his regrets at refusing her kind offer, but before he could say anything, she leaned even closer to him, put a hand on his, and said quietly, "I know someone is trying to kill you, señor."

Now that was a surprise. He kept his face impassive and asked, "What makes you think that?"

"Because that pig Joshua Gullen came in mere moments after you did and looked around until he saw you. It is well known in certain quarters that Gullen will kill a man for a very reasonable price."

Longarm had noticed the lantern-jawed gent who had sauntered into the cantina not long after he did and wondered if the hombre was the one who'd tried to ambush him. Now Mercedes had confirmed that hunch.

Unless she was part of it and was trying to pull some sort of trick . . .

No, Longarm told himself, there was such a thing as being too suspicious. The folks who wanted him dead would have had no way of knowing that he'd duck into this cantina when he avoided their bushwhack attempt. They couldn't have planted Mercedes here ahead of time to trap him.

"I ain't sayin' you're right," he told her, "but let's say you are . . . How do you figure we can get out of here without that fella followin' us?"

"You will come with me?"

Leaving on his own would be just the same as stepping out into a hornet's nest again. He had no way of knowing if Gullen was working alone or if the gunman had allies lurking outside.

"I'll come with you," he told Mercedes. "You seem to know what you're doing."

She stood up and he followed suit. They walked toward

the rear of the cantina. Her brothers were sitting at one of the tables, taking a break from their guitar playing and having a drink. One of them stood up and spoke softly to Mercedes in swift Spanish as she and Longarm passed the table. Longarm caught the name "Gullen" in her reply, so he thought she was probably telling her brothers to keep an eye on the hired killer.

She took his hand and led him through an arched doorway covered with a beaded curtain. The beads clattered behind them as they passed through. They were in a short hallway with a door on each side. Mercedes took him through the door on the left.

"People think there is no way out back here, but they are wrong," she said. She pushed aside a tapestry and revealed a narrow opening, little more than a slit in the adobe wall. She slid through it and Longarm followed, turning sideways to do so. Even then, he barely fit.

They came to a square, open space about as big as a chimney. Enough light came through the slit so Longarm could barely make out a line of round posts set into the adobe of one wall. They stuck out about eight inches and formed the handholds and footholds of a crude ladder.

"Whoever built this building a hundred years ago put these in, in case he needed to escape from the Indians or other enemies," Mercedes whispered. "That is what I believe, anyway. There is no way to know for certain."

She put a hand on one of the posts, ready to climb, but Longarm stopped her with a hand on her shoulder.

"I'll go first," he said. "What's at the top?"

"A trapdoor that opens onto the roof. The buildings are close enough together that we can jump from roof to roof."

Longarm nodded, knowing she was right about that. The old adobe structures were crowded together in this neighborhood of San Antonio known as La Villita, the Little Village. It was one of the oldest parts of town, and, fittingly enough, he had come here tonight looking for an old man.

He pushed that thought out of his mind. He could worry about finding Gonzago later, once he got out of the trap that

Gullen and who knows who else had laid for him.

He started climbing, pulling his rangy body up from post to post. It wasn't easy in these close quarters, but he managed. He wanted to be the first one out of the trapdoor just in case Gullen had somebody watching the cantina's roof. He didn't want Mercedes walking right into a bullet meant for him.

His head bumped the trapdoor, pushing down the crown of his hat a little. It was too dark to see anything up here, so he fumbled around for the latch and found it after a moment. He slid back the latch. A leather strap was nailed to the inside of the trapdoor. He grasped it and pushed up. The strap kept the door from falling open with a crash as he climbed out.

Nobody took a shot at him right away, which was always a good thing. His head was above the level of the low wall around the edge of the cantina's roof. He looked around, scanning the roofs of the nearby buildings. Starlight scattered across them. Longarm didn't see any lurking bushwhackers.

He climbed the rest of the way out of the shaft and lowered the trapdoor to the roof. "Come on up," he called softly through the opening to Mercedes.

As she climbed, he reached over and slid the Colt .44 from the cross-draw rig on his left hip, just in case. A gun never did anybody a damned bit of good while it was still in the holster.

Tumbled raven curls emerged from the opening, followed by the rest of the beautiful young woman. Mercedes stepped over to Longarm and said, "All right, Custis, we can—"

The whipcrack of a rifle shot split the peaceful night. Longarm saw the gout of flame from the muzzle at the same time as he heard Mercedes cry out softly in pain. She started to fall, but his left arm went around her and held her up. His right thrust out the Colt, which roared and bucked in his hand as he squeezed off two swift shots in return.

Longarm's instinctive aim was accurate. A man lunged

up from behind a chimney on an adjoining roof. The rifle he held slipped from his hands and fell with a clatter. He staggered to one side, clutching his midsection, and then toppled over the edge of the building, screaming as he fell. A loud thud cut off that scream.

"Mercedes?" Longarm said.

"I'm all right," she told him. "Let's go, Custis, quickly! Over there!"

She waved a hand at one of the other buildings. Longarm didn't know how badly she was hurt, but he figured she probably didn't need to be jumping from rooftop to rooftop.

He holstered his gun and swept her up in his arms.

"Custis!" she gasped. "You can't—"

"Hide and watch," he said.

She wasn't exactly a slender girl, but he cradled her against him like she was a doll as he bounded to the top of the wall on the cantina roof and leaped across a yard of open space. Even carrying Mercedes, he was able to make the jump and stay on his feet as he landed on the other building.

Somewhere behind him, a man yelled a curse and ordered, "Get around the building! *Around!* Find that son of a bitch!"

"Do I keep goin' in the same direction?" he asked Mercedes."

"*Sí.* On the third building there will be an outside stairway leading down to the street."

More shouts rang out behind them, in both English and Spanish. Longarm thought he heard the thud of fists on flesh. He wondered if Mercedes' brothers were taking a hand in the fight, providing a distraction so that he and Mercedes could get away.

When he reached the building with the stairway, she said, "I can walk. The bullet barely creased my arm."

"Now you tell me," Longarm said with a grin. He lowered her to her slipper-clad feet. As he started down the stairs, he added, "Stay behind me."

It was a good thing she did, because at that moment the

dark shadow of a man appeared at the bottom of the stairs. Longarm saw starlight glint off a gun barrel. His hand flashed to the Colt, and even though the other man already had his gun drawn, the two reports sounded at almost the same instant as both of them fired.

Longarm's shot was more accurate. It drilled the gunman's body and sent him spinning off his feet while the would-be killer's slug slammed into the wall and sent adobe dust flying.

Longarm grabbed Mercedes' hand. Together they ran down the adobe steps built into the wall. She tugged him along an alley, and he went willingly. She hadn't given him any reason not to trust her so far. In fact, she might well have saved his life by helping him get out of the cantina.

Minutes later, after twisting through the maze of streets and alleys in La Villita, Mercedes led him to a small adobe house with a thatched roof portal and vigas protruding from the upper edges of the walls. The sounds of pursuit had died out behind them. They went inside. Mercedes eased the heavy door closed behind them.

"Do you have a match?" she asked Longarm.

He thought her voice sounded a little more strained now. He fished a lucifer out of his vest pocket and snapped it to life with an iron-hard thumbnail. The sudden glare revealed a room that was simply but comfortably furnished.

The light also showed Longarm the blood that ran down Mercedes' left arm and dripped from her fingers. "Good Lord, girl!" he exclaimed.

"It is nothing," she said with a weak smile. "Just a—"

Before she could say "scratch," her eyes rolled up in their sockets and she dropped like a rock.

Chapter 2

Longarm had spotted a lamp sitting on a small, rough-hewn table, so the first thing he did was to go over to it and hold the match flame to the wick. It caught quickly, and when he lowered the lamp's glass chimney, a yellow glow filled the room.

There was no bed in this room, but a door had a beaded curtain over it like the one in the cantina. Carrying the lamp, Longarm pushed the beads aside and saw a small bedroom. He set the lamp back on the table and bent to pick up Mercedes.

She was limp, unconscious. He carried her into the bedroom, brushing the strands of beads aside, and laid her on the bed. He was going to get blood on the covers, but he couldn't help that. Needing better light, he went back into the other room, picked up the lamp, and carried it into the bedroom. A small shelf was attached to the wall beside the bed. He placed the lamp on it.

The blood that had flowed down Mercedes' smooth brown skin had come from a gash on the outside of her upper left arm. Longarm pulled the crimson-stained blouse down to get a better look at the wound, and that exposed Mercedes' left breast. Under other circumstances, Longarm would have enjoyed taking a nice long look at the firm

globe crowned with a large, dark brown nipple, but now he
barely gave it a glance.

A table in one corner of the room held a basin of water.
He took his handkerchief and got it wet, then began swab-
bing the blood off of her arm. Relief went through him as
he saw that the bullet wound really wasn't very deep. It was
a crease, as she had said, but it had bled freely and she had
passed out from the shock of being shot and the blood she
had lost. Longarm was confident that she would be all right,
though.

He looked around in the other room and found a jug. He
pulled the cork and took a sniff at the contents. With a grin,
he lifted the jug to his lips and took a swig of some fiery
tequila.

He found a clean cloth, soaked it with the tequila, and
used it to wipe out the wound. As the tequila bit into the
raw flesh, Mercedes' breath hissed between her teeth. Her
eyes popped open.

"Custis!" she gasped. "What are you doing to me?"

"Cleaning that bullet wound on your arm," he told her.
"Just lie still and let me finish." As he wiped away the last
of the blood from her skin, he went on, "I'm afraid I, uh,
tore up one of your petticoats to get some clean cloth. I'm
gonna have to finish the job by makin' bandages out of it."

She nodded and said, "Do what you have to do. *Gracias*
for taking care of me."

"Well, I reckon it's the least I can do, seein' as how you
got shot on account of me. Gullen must've had some hombres workin' with him."

"We can talk about that later." She looked down at her
bare left breast and asked, "Was it necessary to tear my
clothes half off to tend to my wound?"

"That was sort of an accident," Longarm began.

"This isn't." She shrugged her other shoulder so the
blouse slipped off that breast as well, and she smiled up at
him.

Longarm tried to keep his mind on what he was doing as
he tore more strips off the petticoat he'd found and used

them to bind up her wound. It wasn't easy, though, with those two slowly hardening nipples jutting up at him.

"There," he said as he tied the last strip of bandage in place. "That ought to heal up just fine as long as you keep it clean. It's gonna leave a scar, though."

She shook her head. "I don't care. Scars just show that a person has lived life fully. I think you probably have a number of scars on your body, Custis."

"More than my share," he said. "If you want to know why Gullen was tryin' to kill me—"

She reached up and silenced him by putting her fingers on his lips, brushing the curling longhorn mustache as she did so. "Later," she said as she slid her hand around to the back of his neck and pulled his head down to hers. She whispered, "You can tell me all about that later."

She bounced back mighty quick from being shot, Longarm thought as he pressed his lips to hers and she returned the kiss with a passionate urgency. His left hand came up and cupped her right breast. Its solid weight felt good against his palm. His thumb found the erect nipple and stroked it.

Her mouth opened under his and their tongues met, dueling hotly. They darted back and forth, almost like the dance she had done back in the cantina.

Mercedes took the hand caressing her breast and moved it down under her long skirt. Her legs parted as she pressed Longarm's hand against the thickly furred mound at the juncture of her thighs. He stroked through the silky hair until his middle finger found the slick, hot wetness of her opening. He slid his finger into her, and Mercedes sighed with pleasure and shifted her hips, lifting them slightly from the bed so he could delve even more deeply inside her.

"Custis, I need you," she breathed.

"Are you sure you're up to this?" he asked. "You just got shot about fifteen minutes ago, you know."

"Right now I don't even feel it," she told him. The muscles inside her squeezed his invading finger. "All I feel is this. There is no better cure for whatever is wrong with you."

Longarm couldn't argue with that.

Over the next few minutes, they tended to the business of getting rid of all the unwanted clothes between them. When Mercedes was naked except for the bandages around her wounded arm, she sat on the edge of the bed and used her good arm to pull down the bottoms of Longarm's long underwear, which was all he still had on.

That freed his erect manhood, and Mercedes' eyes widened as she took in the thick, heavy length of his cock.

"Custis, you are much of a man," she said. She stroked him with her right hand, which couldn't come close to going all the way around the pole of male flesh by itself.

He said, "Since you're hurt, I reckon it might be better if I was on the bottom. That way you can keep any pressure off that wounded arm."

"It's not my arm I'm worried about," she said with a little laugh. "If I sit on that thing, it's liable to come all the way up to my throat and choke me!"

He smiled. "Only one way to find out."

Mercedes threw aside the covers that had gotten blood on them while he was tending to her injury. Longarm stretched out on his back with his iron-hard shaft jutting up from his groin like a flagpole. She straddled him, planting a knee on either side of his hips, and reached around behind her to grasp his cock.

She brought the head to her already drenched opening, where it slid in easily. Slowly, inch by inch, she lowered her hips on him. The thick shaft spread her open as he entered her.

"I'm not sure I can . . . take it all," she gasped.

She kept working at it until she did, though. Finally she had all of him buried deep inside her.

"I was . . . right . . . Almost in . . . my throat."

She closed her eyes and tipped her head back in pure pleasure as she began to rock her hips back and forth. Her sex was so tight and hot around him, Longarm had to clench his teeth to fight down the urge to explode and empty himself inside her right away.

Instead he reached up and cupped her breasts, strumming the nipples. She rested her hands on his broad chest to brace herself as her hips began to pump harder. Her ripe red mouth was slack with lust.

Longarm met her movements with thrusts of his own. The heat they generated seemed to fill the room like a furnace. As Mercedes began to buck harder, he moved his hands from her breasts to her hips so he could hold on tight and steady her.

Both of them were so caught up in their lovemaking that it couldn't last long. Longarm felt his climax boiling up inside him and knew he couldn't hold it back. When he felt the spasms of Mercedes' culmination begin to ripple through her body, he didn't try to. He let go, too, driving up into her as deeply as he could while he filled her with his flood.

She cried out as she shuddered, lost in her own climax. When it was finally over, she sagged forward on his chest and kissed him again. His shaft throbbed a final time inside her. Mercedes sighed in contentment against his mouth.

She lifted her head and whispered, "I am so glad you came into the cantina tonight, Custis. When I saw you, I decided I was dancing only for you. Did you know that? The other men, they could watch, but the dance was for you."

"I appreciate that," he said. "Along with everything else you've done for me tonight."

"No more than you have done for me," she said as she snuggled her face against his neck. When he started to move a little, she said quickly, "No! Leave it in me, as long as it will stay."

Longarm was glad to oblige her.

He stroked her back and her hips, and the smooth warmth of her skin felt so good under his hands that his shaft didn't soften all that much despite his climax. He had promised to tell her what all the trouble was about, why somebody had hired Joshua Gullen to kill him. Although he couldn't be *sure* just yet that the case that had brought him here to San Antonio was the reason, it made the most sense. This seemed like as good a time as any to fill her in on the details.

Which he would have done, if a tiny snore hadn't come from her lips just then.

Damned if she hadn't gone to sleep lying on top of him, with his cock still buried inside her!

Longarm grinned as he looked up at the ceiling. He might not be able to tell Mercedes about it right now, but he couldn't stop his own thoughts from going back a couple of days to the office of the chief marshal in Denver . . .

Chapter 3

"San Antonio," Billy Vail said as he put a stack of papers on the desk in front of him.

Longarm had just taken one of his three-for-a-nickel cheroots from his vest pocket. He bit off the end, spat it onto the floor next to the chair of red morocco leather where he sat in front of Vail's desk, and set fire to the gasper with a lucifer he scratched into life on the sole of his left boot, which was cocked on his right knee. He blew a smoke ring toward the banjo clock on the wall and asked, "What about it?"

"I know good and well you've been there." Vail's round, cherubic face was pink and shining with sweat this morning. The windows were open, but there wasn't a breath of fresh air in Denver. It had been like that for a week, and Longarm was going to be glad for any excuse to get out of town.

"Yeah, several times," he admitted.

"You know about the Alamo."

Longarm snorted. "Who doesn't?"

"Yeah, but there are a bunch of other old missions in San Antonio," Vail went on. "I'm sending you to one of them."

Longarm frowned and asked, "You think I need to get religion, Billy? I'll admit, maybe I ain't quite as pious as I should be sometimes—"

"Shut up." Vail mopped sweat off his forehead with a colorful handkerchief he pulled from his pocket. These days, he didn't exactly look like the hard-riding, hell-roaring lawman he had been in his younger days, but he could still put the steel in his voice when he wanted to.

Longarm shut up.

"Before you leave, pick up the end of that cigar you spit on the floor," Vail said. "Henry'll bitch about it if you don't."

"Sure, Billy," Longarm murmured. "Now, what's this about San Antonio and the missions they got down there?"

"Mission San Jose," Vail said as he shoved the papers across the desk to Longarm. "Built about the same time as Mission San Antonio de Valero, which is now better known as the Alamo. There are five missions in town, and I think it's the biggest one. You're going there to investigate a theft."

Longarm hadn't picked up the reports from Vail's desk yet. He preferred having his boss fill him in verbally, although he would take the paperwork with him to study on the train whenever he got a new assignment.

At Vail's comment, he cocked an eyebrow and asked, "Somebody been stealin' pennies from the poor box, Billy? I don't hardly see how that's the business of the federal government."

The chief marshal restrained his impatience and annoyance with a visible effort. "It's a lot more than pennies from the poor box. Somebody stole the Star of Father Cristobal."

"Never heard of it."

"You would have if you'd read the damn reports."

"Why don't you just tell me about it, Billy?" Longarm suggested as mildly as possible.

"Fine," Vail said, although he didn't sound like he thought it was all that fine. "It's a five-pointed star made of silver, about yay big." He held up his pudgy hands about six inches apart.

"Pure silver?"

"So I'm told."

Longarm nodded, impressed. "Dingus must be worth a pretty penny."

"And as if the silver's not enough to make it valuable, there's a jewel mounted in a gold setting at each point of the star."

Longarm let out a low whistle. "And whoever owns this was keepin' it at a church, you say?"

"The Catholic Church owns it. Where else would they keep it? It's a religious relic. This Father Cristobal had it made about a hundred and fifty years ago, not long after the missions in San Antonio were founded. The silver came from mines in Mexico, the gold for the mountings from the lost mine of the San Saba."

Longarm had heard of the lost San Saba mine. Located somewhere in central Texas, it had been worked by Indians who'd been enslaved by the priests and the Spanish soldiers who had come to the New World to "civilize" it. Eventually those slaves had risen against the outsiders and slaughtered them, and ever since then, no one had ever been able to find the old mine, although many had searched for it.

"Does this have anything to do with findin' the San Saba, Billy?" Longarm asked. "Because if it does, I got a hunch that's a fool's errand."

Vail shook his head. "No, that's not what's going on here. It's just a coincidence that's where the gold came from."

"What about the jewels?"

Vail shrugged. "There's no telling where they came from. That information's been lost somewhere in history."

"All right, I can see where something that's worth that much would need to be tracked down," Longarm said with a nod, "but I still don't understand why I'm supposed to do the trackin'. We don't work for the Catholic Church."

"No, we still work for Uncle Sam's Justice Department," Vail snapped. "Just be quiet for a minute and I'll explain it."

Longarm puffed on his cheroot and waited.

"A while back, the Mexican government started making

noises about how the Star of Father Cristobal ought to belong to Mexico. They sent letters to the Church asking that the Star be sent to a mission in Mexico City."

"Seems like with all the uproar that's always goin' on down there, they'd have more important things to worry about," Longarm muttered.

"Yeah, but the Star's worth a lot of money, and no matter who's in charge south of the border, they always seem to be strapped for cash. Maybe more importantly, though, it's a matter of pride. Since Texas used to be part of Mexico, you know how touchy they are about things they think ought to still belong to them."

Longarm leaned forward and said, "Wait a minute, Billy. Are you tellin' me you think somebody workin' for the Mexican government stole this Star of Father Cristobal?"

"I don't know who stole it," Vail said, "but somebody in Washington thinks that's a possibility. That's where you come in. The State Department is involved in delicate negotiations with the Mexican government right now, and they don't want anything upsetting the apple cart. So they asked the Justice Department to ask us to send somebody down there to find out exactly what happened and who's responsible for it."

"The State Department's always negotiatin' delicately with somebody. What's this about?"

"I don't have any idea, and that part of it is none of our business, anyway," Vail said. "All they want you to do, Custis, is go down there, find out what happened to that relic, and get it back if you can."

Longarm frowned. That part of the job was straightforward enough, he supposed, but there was a considerable amount of murkiness around the edges, and he never had cottoned much to operating in the dark.

Still, he wasn't in the habit of turning down assignments and he didn't intend to start now.

"I reckon I can do that," he said. "If I get my hands on the Star, do I take it back to the mission in San Antone?"

"That's right."

"Where, since somebody already stole it once, it might get stole again?"

"That's not our lookout."

"I reckon not." Longarm put the cheroot in his mouth and picked up the reports from Vail's desk. He tapped them on the desk to straighten them. "Henry's got my travel vouchers?"

"That's right."

Longarm stood up, straightening to his full six-foot-plus height. "I'll be on my way, then."

"You'll have to be careful on this one, Custis," Vail added. "You'll be dealing with the Catholic Church and quite possibly a foreign government. Remember you're representing the United States in this matter. You can't just go busting in with your usual bull-in-a-china-shop methods."

Longarm grinned around the cheroot. "Ah, hell, Billy, don't worry. I'll be just as gentle and sensitive as a little lamb."

"Lord help us," Vail muttered as Longarm left the office.

Henry, the bespectacled youngster who played the typewriter in the chief marshal's outer office, was waiting for Longarm. He held out an envelope.

"Travel vouchers, train tickets, and expense money, Marshal," he said.

Longarm took the envelope and stuffed it in an inside pocket in his coat. "Much obliged, Henry. By the way, the end of this cigar is layin' on the floor beside the red leather chair in there. Billy told me to pick it up, but I plumb forgot to do it."

Henry's pale face stiffened. "I'm not employed here as a janitor, you know. I'm Marshal Vail's secretary."

"Yeah, I kinda figured that out after all this time." Longarm snagged his hat off the hat tree just inside the door. "I'll go back and get it . . ."

"No, no, that's all right," Henry said with a wave of his hand and a sigh of resignation. "I'll tend to it in a moment. You have a train to catch in an hour."

Longarm put his hat on. "Reckon I'd better rattle my

hocks, then. Don't melt away to nothin' in this heat while I'm gone."

"Don't sound so superior," Henry said. "It's probably even hotter in San Antonio than it is here."

Longarm frowned. "I hadn't thought about that," he admitted. When it came to heat, Texas was usually hotter than just about any place short of Death Valley. "So long, Henry."

He left the office and the federal building and headed for his rented room on the other side of Cherry Creek. He had just about enough time to gather up his possibles, pack his war bag, and make the train station.

An hour later, he was on a southbound out of Denver, heading for Santa Fe and ultimately El Paso.

Chapter 4

There was no direct way of traveling from Denver to San Antonio without getting on a horse and riding, but that was a lot slower despite being shorter. Longarm took the Denver & Rio Grande to El Paso, where, after a six-hour layover, he boarded an eastbound Southern Pacific train that would take him to San Antonio.

He spent most of that six-hour stop in a saloon he knew of near the depot, sipping Maryland rye and joining in a friendly poker game. It was early morning when he left El Paso, and he dozed all the way to San Antonio. He had been to West Texas often enough to know that he wouldn't be missing much in the way of scenery. The sleep would do him more good.

It was four o'clock in the afternoon when he reached San Antonio, but at this time of year the sun wouldn't go down for another four hours yet. Since there was plenty of daylight left, after Longarm had rented a hotel room and dropped off his rifle and war bag, he found a livery stable and rented a horse as well for the ride out to Mission San Jose.

If he had known he was going to be in San Antonio for a long time or would be taking a long ride, he would have gone to Fort Sam Houston and requisitioned a horse from their remount. But since he didn't know yet, it seemed to make more sense to rent a horse and put the cost on his expense account.

All five of the missions were located along the San Antonio River, a narrow, twisting stream that ran through the heart of the settlement. San Jose was several miles south of downtown, Longarm had learned from reading the reports he had brought with him. All he had to do was follow the river.

He couldn't miss the huge stone church sitting in a broad, grassy compound west of the stream. It had a tall bell tower in the front, with an even taller domed roof behind it. A mighty impressive-looking place, Longarm thought as he rode up to it.

Beds of bright-colored flowers surrounded the church, along with green lawns and carefully tended shrubbery. Longarm swung down from the rented horse and looped its reins around an iron hitching post, then followed a flagstone walk past an old well to the church's front door.

Someone must have seen him coming. One of the massive wooden double doors swung open, and a brown-robed priest with a narrow face and graying dark hair stepped out.

"Can I help you, my son?" he asked.

"I'm lookin' for whoever's in charge here," Longarm said.

The priest inclined his head to indicate that was him. "I am Father Tomás."

"My name is Custis Long." Longarm lowered his voice. He didn't see anybody hanging around eavesdropping, but his years as a lawman had ingrained caution in him. "I need to talk to you about the Star of Father Cristobal."

Father Tomás's eyes widened slightly. "Of course," he murmured. "Please follow me."

He led Longarm into the church but turned to go down a short hallway before they entered the sanctuary itself. Longarm followed him into a room that was furnished as both an office and a library, with scores of volumes bound in dark leather on the shelves that lined the walls.

Father Tomás left the door open behind them and turned to face Longarm. His voice held a sharp edge as he asked, "Have you come to ransom the Star?"

"Hold on a minute," Longarm said. He had almost called the priest "old son," but he thought that might be disrespectful. "I'm not the one who *took* that relic of yours. I'm the hombre who's supposed to *find* it. Deputy U.S. Marshal Custis Long."

He reached inside his coat and brought out the leather folder that contained his badge and bona fides. Father Tomás looked at the identification and nodded.

"My apologies, Marshal," he said. "I admit that since the theft, I've been a bit on edge." He motioned toward a heavy armchair with a high back in front of the desk. "Won't you sit down? Would you like something to drink? A glass of wine?"

Longarm shook his head. "I'm obliged for the offer, but I reckon I'll pass. What I'd like is to hear about the Star and how it got itself stole."

"Of course." The priest settled down in a similar chair behind the desk. "I was hoping the government would send someone, but I wasn't sure if they would or not. This is more of a religious matter."

"Robbery's robbery, no matter what gets stole," Longarm said. "And from what I hear, both the U.S. and Mexican governments are a mite touchy about the Star of Father Cristobal."

"Yes, and it doesn't belong to either of them, no matter how much they argue about it. It's a holy relic of the Church. Do you know anything about the Star, Marshal?"

"Just that it was made by an old padre called Father Cristobal about a hundred and fifty years ago, and it's worth a whole heap of money."

Father Tomás smiled thinly. "Yes, and money usually trumps religion, doesn't it?"

"The unkind might say the two go hand in hand."

"And all too often, they would be right. But in this case, the Star of Father Cristobal has a value over and above a monetary one. It was made to commemorate a miracle."

Longarm had never placed a whole lot of stock in miracles, but he kept his face neutral and said, "Go on."

"Father Cristobal was sent here from Mexico City to replace another priest," Father Tomás said. "The mule train he was traveling with was attacked by savage Indians, and he was separated from the others and forced to flee for his life into the mountains. Finally, after much danger and hardship, he reached San Antonio, alone and on foot, nearly dead. But he claimed that God had protected him, and in time he recovered. He said that God had come to him in the form of a star that guided him, and so he had a silver star made and decorated it with jewels to honor the Lord."

Longarm nodded. "It's a nice story, all right."

"You do not believe, Marshal?"

"I didn't say that. I wasn't there, Father, so I don't know what happened. But in the words of the old hymn, farther along we'll know more about it."

"Indeed," Father Tomás murmured. "It certainly seems like a miracle to me that one old man was able to travel hundreds of miles, alone and on foot, through some of the harshest territory in the world, and survive."

"I can't argue about that," Longarm admitted. "But now that you've given me the history of the . . . relic—" He had almost called it a dingus again. "—I need some practical details, like where it was being kept when it disappeared."

Father Tomás got to his feet and held out a hand. "Of course. Come with me. I'll show you."

He took Longarm into the sanctuary with its high, vaulted, echoing ceiling and pointed to a niche cut into one of the stone walls.

"The Star was on display here," the priest said, "as it has been for more than a hundred years."

Longarm looked around. "Where anybody could just walk in and pick it up?"

"Where the faithful could see it and take comfort in its message that God is always watching over us."

Longarm tugged on his right earlobe and then scraped

his thumbnail along his jawline as he frowned in thought. "Is the place locked up at night?"

"This is a church, Marshal," Father Tomás said in a gently chiding voice. "Would you lock God's people out of His house?"

Longarm suppressed the impulse to exclaim "Hell's bells!" or some such. Instead he said, "So what you're tellin' me is that anybody could've waltzed in here anytime and taken that silver star?"

"Well . . . if you want to look at it like that . . . I suppose what you say is correct."

Longarm was tempted to take the first train out of San Antonio, go back to Denver, and tell Billy Vail that the job was impossible. There were thousands and thousands of suspects, and no way to narrow them down.

"But the Star has been here for more than a hundred years, and no one has ever bothered it," Father Tomás went on. "How were we to know that someone would steal it now?"

"I suppose you've got a point there, padre."

"Do you think you can find it, Marshal?"

Longarm wanted to tell him there wasn't a chance in hell, but of course he couldn't do that. Instead he said, "I'll do my best."

Father Tomás smiled. "That's all anyone can do."

"When was the Star taken?"

"Ten days ago." The answer was immediate. "I'm certain of that. It was here Saturday night, but gone when I came in for early mass that Sunday morning."

In ten days, the thief could have gone almost anywhere. But when a chore was already the next thing to impossible, what did one more difficulty matter?

"Did you see anybody skulkin' around Saturday night, anybody who looked suspicious or wasn't usually here?"

"People come and go all the time to pray," Father Tomás said, sweeping a hand at the pews and the altar. "Many of them I know from the parish, but there are always strangers, as well."

"So you didn't notice anybody unusual?"

The priest shook his head. "No, I'm afraid not."

Longarm managed not to sigh in frustration. "What about the other folks who were here at the mission? I might need to talk to them and find out if they saw anything."

"Whatever you like, Marshal, but I don't think you'll find out anything from them. They're very simple people. Peasants. I doubt if they notice anything beyond the task at hand."

"Well, we'll see. Is it all right if I sort of wander around the grounds?"

"Of course. This is the Lord's house, and you are one of the Lord's children, are you not?"

"I don't know. I'm such a scoundrel He may have disowned me by now."

"I doubt that, Marshal. I seriously doubt it." Father Tomás paused. "Please, let me know if there's anything else I can do to help you."

Longarm left the priest in the sanctuary and walked back outside. It was late afternoon by now, but a sultry heat still lay over the landscape. Henry had been right. It was even hotter in Texas than it was in Colorado, although surrounded by all the green grass and trees and flowers, somehow it didn't *seem* quite as sweltering here on the grounds of Mission San Jose.

The mission compound contained several outbuildings, some of adobe, some of stone, and the cultivated fields nearby were probably part of it, too. Longarm saw a few other houses in the area, and he had passed several businesses—a livery stable and blacksmith shop, a general store, and a couple of saloons—about half a mile back up the road. On the other side of the river lay more farmland. It was a nice, peaceful area.

As he started walking around the church, he passed one of the long flower beds. A man in a white shirt, white trousers, and a straw sombrero stood at the edge of the flagstone walk with a rake in his hands. He'd been tending to the flowers, raking the dirt between the plants and removing

fallen leaves and petals. He paid no attention to Longarm as
the big lawman walked past.

Or so Longarm thought, until the man said softly,
"Señor?"

Longarm stopped. "What can I do for you, amigo?"

"You are a lawman. You have come to find the Star of
Father Cristobal."

The blunt declaration took Longarm by surprise. He
thought back to his arrival at Mission San Jose a short time
earlier. This fella might have been working around the front
of the building; Longarm wasn't sure about that. But even if
he had been within earshot, Longarm had introduced himself to Father Tomás by name only and hadn't revealed his
identity as a deputy U.S. marshal until they were inside.

But he *had* mentioned the Star of Father Cristobal, he
recalled, and not only that, the priest had left the door of the
office open while they talked.

Longarm glanced down at the feet of the man with the
rake. The man wore rope-soled sandals, and Longarm had a
hunch he could move around in them pretty quietly when
he wanted to. The workers here at the mission probably
weren't quite as simple, childlike, and innocent as Father
Tomás wanted to be believe they were.

"You have something you want to tell me, amigo?"
Longarm asked.

The man gave a quick glance around and then said quietly, "Talk to Gonzago. He can help you."

Chapter 5

The man's broad, dark face testified to his Indian heritage. Longarm studied him for a moment, then, deciding that the man was sincere, asked, "Who's Gonzago?"

"An old man who works here. He drives a wagon that carries fruits and vegetables from the fields to the market in San Antonio. We grow more here than we can use, so the priests sell it in the market and the money goes to the Church."

"Does Gonzago live here at the mission? Where can I find him?"

The man shook his head. "He lives in La Villita. You know it?"

Longarm had heard of the neighborhood, south of downtown and the Alamo. "I know it," he said. "Do you know exactly where Gonzago's house is?"

Again the man shook his head. "No, but if you ask, people will tell you where to find him."

"What does Gonzago know about the Star of Father Cristobal? Is he the one who stole it?"

The man crossed himself and said, "*Dios mio*! Gonzago, steal from the Church? Never, señor! Sometimes I think he is more devout than the priests themselves. But he is a scholar and knows much about its history."

"A scholar," Longarm repeated. "Who drives a produce wagon . . ."

The man with the rake frowned. "A man's job is not always who he is, señor."

"I reckon that's true. Tell me more about Gonzago."

"He is an educated man. He came here from Mexico City, and no one knows what he did there. It would not surprise me if he taught at the university. But I know he could read the words on the back of the Star of Father Cristobal."

That caught Longarm's attention more than anything else he had heard so far. Nobody had said anything about the relic he was looking for having words on the back of it.

"What words? Were they carved in the silver?"

The man nodded. "*Sí*, señor. Very faint. The years have worn them down. But Gonzago saw them, and he could read them."

"Written in Latin, I reckon." Longarm nodded, too, thinking that he would ask Father Tomás what the words said.

"No, señor. Not Latin. An unknown tongue the priests cannot read."

"But Gonzago can?" That seemed mighty unlikely to Longarm.

"*Sí*, señor. I speak the truth."

"Did Gonzago ever tell you what the words say?"

"No. He would not speak of it except to say that they were very important words."

This whole thing was sounding more and more loco, Longarm thought, but it wasn't like he had a lot to go on. The trail was already cold, so he couldn't afford to pass up anything that might possibly help him track down the stolen relic.

"All right, thanks, amigo," he said. "I'll talk to this Gonzago fella. What's your name?"

"Lopez, señor."

"Is it all right if I tell Gonzago what you told me about him?"

"Of course. But if it is all right with you, I would rather you did not say anything to Father Tomás."

"Why's that?" Longarm asked.

"He is a good man, but he thinks no one but the priests know anything about what really goes on here. The servants would like to keep it that way, señor."

Longarm had to grin. The folks in charge thought they knew more than they really did, and the ones who did the actual work of the world knew a hell of a lot more than any of the higher-ups ever gave them credit for.

"You got it, Señor Lopez," he said. "I'll keep my mouth shut."

"*Gracias*."

Longarm asked Lopez if he had seen anybody unusual around the mission on the night the Star had been stolen, but the man shook his head. "Think you could ask around amongst the other folks who work here?" Longarm asked.

"You mean like I would be your deputy?"

"Something like that," Longarm allowed.

"Of course. I will be discreet about it."

"*Muchas gracias* to you, my friend."

The sun was low in the western sky by the time Longarm had followed the river back to downtown San Antonio. He rode past the Menger Hotel, which was next door to the old Alamo mission and the nicest place to stay in the city. Nice enough that Henry would have balked at the cost of it on Longarm's expense account if he had stayed there, so he had rented a room at a smaller hotel a few blocks away.

He took the horse back to the livery stable. La Villita was in walking distance, so he shouldn't need the mount again tonight, he thought.

Before he looked up the old man called Gonzago, though, he needed something to eat. He thought maybe he could slip a meal in the Menger's dining room past Henry when it came time to settle up on his expenses.

Most of the cattle barons in West Texas and South Texas stayed at the fancy hotel when they visited San Antonio, and you could tell it by the excellent steaks they served in their dining room. Longarm had stayed here once with his old friend Jessica Starbuck, the owner of the vast Circle Star Ranch, and he had to smile as he remembered how he and Jessie had put the big, soft four-poster bed in her suite to such good use. If he had any time to spare when this job was over, he would send a wire to Jessie and see if they could get together before he had to head back to Denver.

Night had fallen by the time Longarm strolled out of the Menger and turned south. He crossed the river on an arching stone bridge and headed for La Villita. That was where the town's biggest market was located, along with a number of businesses and many houses packed closely together. Longarm figured the market would still be open, and since Gonzago delivered produce there, that was where he planned to start his search for the old man.

A language that even priests couldn't read, he mused as he walked along streets that were still busy even though the sun was down. He didn't know if he believed that or not. Still, he supposed he couldn't rule it out.

Even if it was true, and even if he found Gonzago and the old man told him what the words on the back of the Star said, that didn't mean the information would help Longarm find the relic. The whole thing might come to nothing. And yet it was a place to start, and since places to start were in short supply, Longarm hoped that finding Gonzago would turn out to be important.

The market took up an entire block in La Villita, and, as Longarm had suspected, it was still open. Lamps burned brightly in many of the stalls that were set up to buy, sell, and trade goods of all sorts. Longarm headed for an area where fruits and vegetables were on display in open baskets. Long strings of colorful peppers hung from the posts that supported the thatched roof.

Longarm nodded and smiled at a middle-aged woman who was working there. She was heavy-set but still pretty, with dark eyes that flashed fire. "*Buenas noches*, señora," he told her.

"You want to buy some melons?" she asked, and he

didn't think she was talking about the ample breasts that pushed out the top of her blouse. "Or some peppers?"

"Not today, I'm afraid, but I'll take one of those apples in that basket there," he said, pointing to them.

"They are very good apples, señor." She handed him one of them. "Grown in the orchards at the Mission San Jose."

That was a lucky break, Longarm thought. "Then old Gonzago must have brought them here in his wagon," he said.

The woman looked a little surprised as she asked, "You know Gonzago?"

"I know of him. In fact, I'd like to talk to him. Do you happen to know where I can find him?" He extended a coin to her. "For the apple."

The money was considerably more than an apple would cost. The woman hesitated before taking it, though. She said, "Gonzago is a harmless old man."

"I know. I mean him no harm. I just want to talk to him."

The woman thought about it a moment longer, then shrugged and reached for the coin. "Three blocks down this street, then a block west. An old house with a rooster on the roof." She revolved a finger. "You know. The thing that shows how the wind blows."

"A weather vane," Longarm said.

"*Sí.* A weather vane."

Longarm thought he could find that place where Gonzago lived, even at night. He polished up the apple on the sleeve of his coat, crunched a bite from it with his strong teeth, and chewed the juicy, flavorful fruit. "*Gracias,*" he told the woman. "' *Sta bueno.*"

As he turned around, he saw a skinny man with a mustache like a pair of rat tails moving some of the baskets of produce. He supposed the man was the woman's husband, which she confirmed by yelling at him in Spanish, calling him *estupido*, and telling him he was arranging the baskets all wrong.

Following the directions the woman had given him, Longarm left the market. When he got away from its immediate

area, the streets weren't as busy. Along with fewer people,
there were fewer lights, too, but Longarm could still see
well enough to know where he was going.

He turned into the block where Gonzago was supposed
to live and started looking for a weather vane in the shape
of a rooster. He found it a moment later, revolving lazily in
a gentle breeze atop a tiny adobe cottage.

The house was dark, but Gonzago could have turned in
already. Most old men went to sleep with the chickens.
Longarm went up a short walk made of crushed stone and
flanked on both sides by cactus gardens. He knocked on the
door.

No one answered. He knocked again and called, "Gonzago? Señor? Are you home? I'm a friend. Lopez from
Mission San Jose sent me."

Still no response. Longarm wasn't sure where an old-
timer would be at this time of night except home. Something
unsettled stirred inside him, the lawman's instinct that told
him trouble might be afoot.

He reached across his body with his right hand and
wrapped his fingers around the butt of the .44. His left hand
went to the door latch. The door didn't have a lock, but it
might be barred on the inside.

It wasn't. When Longarm pulled the latch back, the door
opened easily.

He halfway expected somebody to take a shot at him
from the shadows, although he had no reason other than a
gut feeling to think that way. The inside of the house remained dark and quiet, though. He took a step inside the
door and called softly, "Gonzago?"

Again there was no answer.

Longarm took a match from his vest pocket and snapped
it to life. He squinted against the sudden glare of the flame
and looked around. As he expected from the outside of the
cottage, the room was small and simply furnished but neatly
kept.

Except for an overturned chair beside the table. The
chair lay on its side on the hard-packed dirt floor as if

someone had run into it and knocked it over. As fastidious as he appeared to be, judging from the rest of the house, Gonzago would have righted the chair if he had knocked it over.

If he had been able to.

That thought pushed into Longarm's mind and made him bend over, holding the match close to the ground. He swung his arm back and forth, searching, and near the door, he found what he was looking for.

A tiny dark splotch in the dirt that could be where a drop of blood had fallen.

Alarm bells were ringing in Longarm's head now. Quickly, he went through the whole house and didn't find anything else suspicious, but he didn't find Gonzago, either. The old man was gone, and Longarm suspected that someone had taken him out of his home against his will, probably earlier tonight. Longarm thought he remembered Lopez saying that Gonzago had been at the mission earlier in the day.

With his gun still in his hand, Longarm left the cottage. He paused on the walk, between the clumps of cactus, and took a cheroot from his vest pocket. He reached for a match and then stopped short before pulling out a lucifer. If anybody was watching Gonzago's house, striking a light would make him a target.

As it turned out, it didn't really matter, because the next second Colt flame bloomed in the darkness anyway and Longarm felt the wind-rip of a slug as it passed close beside his ear.

Chapter 6

Longarm's reaction was instant. His Colt came up and gouted fire as he squeezed the trigger. He aimed at the muzzle flash but figured the bushwhacker was already on the move.

That was a good guess. Another shot split the night. Lead screamed through the darkness in search of the big lawman.

Longarm was already moving, too. From the corner of his eye he had spotted an empty cart sitting at the edge of the street down the block. He dashed toward it and flung another shot in the direction of the unknown gunman as he ran.

He didn't want to throw lead all over town, though. The houses were crowded in close around here, and there was no telling what—or who—a stray bullet might hit. He wanted to capture whoever was taking those potshots at him so he could ask the varmint some questions, but if he couldn't do that he'd rather give the bushwhacker the slip so no innocent folks would be hurt.

He hoped that hadn't happened already.

When he reached the cart, he ducked into a crouch behind it. It took him only a second to thumb a couple of fresh rounds from his shell belt into the Colt's cylinder to replace the two he had fired. He listened intently.

The street was deserted. Anybody who had been out had ducked for cover when the shooting started. He heard people shouting questions in Spanish, wanting to know what was going on. Somebody would probably send for the law, if they hadn't already.

Longarm usually checked in with the local authorities in whatever town his job took him to. He would have done that here in San Antonio, too, he just hadn't gotten around to it yet.

But he figured if the local star packers showed up now, they would have a lot of questions and he wasn't in much of a mood to spend hours answering them. Maybe it was time for him to get away from Gonzago's house.

A couple of minutes had gone by since the last shot was directed at him. Had the bushwhacker given up and lit a shuck out of La Villita, since his ambush attempt had failed?

Or was he lurking in the shadows, waiting for his quarry to show himself again?

Longarm knew there was only one way to find out. He burst out from behind the cart and made a dash for a darkened doorway across the street. It belonged to some business that was closed for the night.

Another muzzle flash stabbed through the darkness. Longarm felt as much as heard the slug sizzle past his head. The gunman was a good shot. Just not quite good enough . . . so far.

Longarm reached the doorway, which was recessed enough to give him some cover. He pressed himself back into it. As he did so, he heard the rapid patter of retreating footsteps, followed by shouting from the other direction. He saw the glare of lantern light down the street. Men were coming to see what all the shooting was about.

The gunman had cut and run before those men could get here. Longarm was convinced of that. He didn't want to be caught here, either, so he slid out of the doorway and into another shadow. He worked his way along the street, sticking to darkness as much as he could.

But as he did, he felt the skin crawl on the back of his neck. He was being watched. The would-be killer was still out there somewhere, still gunning for him.

He spotted a cantina just up ahead, with the swift notes of guitar music coming from its open door. If the place was crowded, the gunman wouldn't make a try for him there. When Longarm reached the door, he saw that the cantina was busy, all right. Men crowded around most of the tables, and many of them were clapping in time with the music, which came from a pair of guitars being played by two young men who looked enough alike to be twins and probably were.

Longarm slipped into the smoky interior. The gunman might follow him in here and wait for him to leave, then try to kill him again. At least Longarm could catch his breath, though, and maybe get a drink before that happened.

He took a chair at one of the few empty tables. A pretty señorita in a low-cut peasant blouse and long skirt brought him a glass of tequila and a beer. He would have rather had a shot of Maryland rye, but he doubted if they had such a thing in this place. The girl gave him a dazzling smile, too.

But then an even prettier señorita pushed through a beaded curtain over a door at the back of the room and moved into an open space in the center of the floor. The guitar players started up another tune, and the girl began to dance . . .

Sunlight was slanting through a gap in the curtains over the room's single window when Longarm woke up. He usually didn't sleep this late.

He usually didn't wake up with a beautiful young woman stroking her soft hands up and down his hard cock, either, but that seemed to be what was going on this morning.

Still naked except for the makeshift bandage around her arm, Mercedes was curled up on the bed next to Longarm with her head next to his groin. She lifted herself enough so she could reach the head of his shaft and started licking it with little strokes of her tongue. Longarm couldn't hold back a groan of pleasure.

She paused in what she was doing and looked up at him with a mischievous smile. "Good morning, Custis," she said. "You slept well?"

"Mighty good," he told her. "But I woke up even better."

"Lie there and relax while I do this for you."

Longarm wasn't just about to argue.

She started stroking his cock with her tongue again, licking the thick pole from crown to base and back up again. Then she gripped it with both hands and took the head in her mouth, closing her warm lips around it as she began to suck gently. Her mouth stretched wider, allowing her to engulf more and more of him, but she couldn't come close to swallowing all of it. She pumped her hands up and down the remainder of the shaft.

Longarm closed his eyes and luxuriated for long moments in the exquisite sensations her lips and tongue sent cascading through him. But then his sense of fair play began to bother him. Mercedes was the one doing all the work, and she had an injured arm, although it didn't seem to be bothering her much this morning.

He reached over, took hold of her hips, and moved her bottom half. She helped him position her so that her thighs were on either side of his head and her belly was pressed to his chest. They managed that without her mouth ever leaving his erect member.

He spread her thighs, revealing the dark thicket of hair around the lips of her sex. Beads of her juices sparkled in the hair. She was wet and got even wetter as Longarm used his thumbs to spread the folds of flesh and speared his tongue between them. It was Mercedes' turn to moan in pleasure, the sound coming from deep inside her and emerging around his cock as she continued to suck it.

He took his tongue away and slid the middle finger of his right hand in her instead, moving it around until it was

well-coated with her slick juices. Then he slid it into the
puckered brown hole between the lush cheeks of her backside. At the same time, he resumed licking her and used his
other hand to find the sensitive nubbin of flesh at the other
end of her opening. He twirled his fingers around it.

That combined assault on her senses was too much for
Mercedes. She cried out and began to buck in a wild climax, and as she raised up and let his cock fall out of her
mouth, Longarm unleashed his own culmination in thick
white jets that flew through the air and landed on her face.
She clamped her thighs on the sides of his head and
gushed her release. It was a wild few seconds, and when it
was over, both of them were a mite messy but wholly
satisfied.

They cuddled together for a while and then cleaned up,
including changing the bandages on Mercedes' wounded
arm. The bullet gash didn't look too bad. Tequila was good
medicine.

They ate tortillas at the little table in the front room.
Mercedes said, "You promised to tell me why Joshua Gullen
and those other men wanted to kill you."

Longarm chuckled. "I was going to last night, but you
up and dozed off on me. And I do mean *on* me."

She gave one of those defiant tosses of her head that
seemed to be a habit with her. "It is not my fault your
lovemaking exhausted me. Besides, I was weak from losing
all that blood."

"Yeah, I know." Longarm's expression grew solemn.
"And I'm sorry you got hurt because of me."

"So tell me why Gullen was after you."

"I'm pretty sure it was because I was tryin' to find an
old man called Gonzago."

Mercedes frowned. "The old *viejo* who delivers produce
to the market from the missions?"

"That's right. You know him?"

She shrugged. "Everyone in La Villita knows Gonzago.
Why is he so important that someone would try to kill you
to keep you from finding him?"

"Because he may know something about the Star of Father Cristobal."

Mercedes shook her head in confusion. "I have heard of it. Some sort of religious relic, is it not?"

"That's right." After everything that had happened, Longarm trusted her, so he said, "Mercedes, I'm a deputy United States marshal."

Her beautiful dark eyes widened.

Longarm went on to tell her about the assignment that had brought him to San Antonio. Dancing in the cantina like she did, she probably heard a lot of rumors that went around town. She might be able to help in other ways besides saving his life from hired killers . . . and giving him a couple of the most pleasurable times he had spent in bed in quite a while.

When he was finished, she said, "Do you believe this story about the writing on the back of the Star of Father Cristobal and how Gonzago was able to read it?"

"I don't know. But somebody sure thinks it's true, because it looked to me like the old-timer was taken from his house by force sometime yesterday evening."

Mercedes' hand rose to her mouth. "No!" she gasped. "Someone hurt old Gonzago?"

"I don't know if he's hurt," Longarm replied, not saying anything about the drop of blood he had found on the ground in Gonzago's cottage. "But I'd bet a hat that the same fella who hired Gullen to kill me is holding Gonzago prisoner. It's too far-fetched to think the reason has something to do with anything except the Star of Father Cristobal."

Mercedes nodded slowly. "Yes, I think you must be right. But how would Gullen know you are searching for the Star? Would he try to kill anyone who showed up at Gonzago's home looking for the old man?"

"I don't know," Longarm replied, "but I've got a pretty good idea who can tell me."

"Who?"

"Joshua Gullen his ownself . . . and I'm hoping that you can tell me where to find him."

Chapter 7

Mercedes stared at him for a long moment before she exclaimed, "Custis, have you gone mad? Last night Gullen tries to kill you, and now you talk about finding him!"

"He's got the answers I need," Longarm said. "Some of 'em, anyway."

"And what makes you think I know where he is?"

"You recognized him in the cantina last night. I'll bet you know a lot about what goes on in San Antonio, and that includes having an idea where a fella would have to go to hire a killer like Gullen."

She gave a stubborn shake of her head. "You were lucky enough to escape from him. It makes no sense to put yourself back in danger by going and looking for him."

"It makes all the sense in the world," Longarm said. "There's an old sayin' about the hunted becoming the hunter. That's just what I intend to do."

"And if I refuse to help you with this madness?"

Longarm shrugged. "Reckon I'll have to start somewhere else. But I intend to find Gullen, and I intend to see to it that he tells me who hired him."

"Because that will lead you to Gonzago."

He nodded. "And there's a good chance whoever has Gonzago also has the Star of Father Cristobal."

Mercedes frowned across the table at him for a long time before she finally sighed and nodded. "I do not know it to be true from personal experience, but I have heard it said that Gullen can be found in a saloon called the Golden Dove."

The name was vaguely familiar to Longarm. He asked, "Where's that?"

"A few blocks north of the Alamo." She paused, then went on, "It is a bad place, Custis. Not just a saloon, but a gambling den and a brothel as well."

"Sort of like that cantina where you work?"

"I dance there!" she said, her eyes flashing fire. "No one fucks me for money!"

"Sorry," Longarm said, and meant it. "I reckon that was a rotten thing to say."

She crossed her arms over her breasts. The dark brown nipples showed plainly through the thin shift she wore. "You will not be able to find Gullen there until tonight," she said. "What do you plan to do in the meantime?"

"Well, I don't rightly know," he drawled. "Seems to me like that's the next step in the plan, so I guess I'll just wait."

She reached across the table and took hold of his hand. "Good. Then you have all day to make up for offending me. You can start by taking me back to bed."

Longarm smiled as he got to his feet. He intended to do his best to oblige her.

The namesake of the Golden Dove perched on top of the awning above the boardwalk in front of the place. It was about four feet tall, probably cast from plaster and covered in gilt paint. Longarm was sure it wasn't actual gold, because if it was, somebody would have stolen it by now. Also, it would have been so heavy it would have come crashing down through that awning.

After leaving Mercedes' neat little house, Longarm had gone back to his hotel and changed clothes, trading the brown tweed suit for a pair of jeans and a well-worn work shirt. He hadn't shaved, so he had a pretty good coating of dark stubble on his cheeks, jaw, and chin. He looked like a drifting cowpoke now. A lot of men wore mustaches—though few had one that curled as luxuriantly as his—so he hoped the difference in his appearance might be enough to keep him from being spotted right away by Gullen.

The Golden Dove had a side door. Longarm entered by it and went to the bar. The place was crowded tonight, which was both an advantage and a disadvantage. It would make it more difficult for him to locate Gullen if the lantern-jawed killer was there.

A balding drink juggler came over and drew a beer for him, then collected the coin Longarm slid across the hardwood. He could have asked the man if Joshua Gullen was around tonight. The bartenders here were probably used to that question if Gullen made the Golden Dove his base of operations.

But that would also call attention to him, and Longarm didn't want that just yet.

Instead he just sipped his beer and unobtrusively studied the occupants of the room in the long mirror behind the bar. He couldn't see all of them, of course, but he had a good look at quite a few of them.

He didn't spot Joshua Gullen anywhere.

Turning, he rested his right elbow on the bar behind him and held the mug of beer in his left as he continued nursing the brew. The mug helped obscure his face. He checked the roulette wheel, the faro layout, the poker tables, and didn't see Gullen around any of the games of chance. The smoky light from the oil lamps barely penetrated to the far corners of the big room, but Longarm studied the men at those tables as well and was convinced none of them was Gullen.

That left two possibilities: Gullen was upstairs with one of the soiled doves who worked at the Golden Dove, or he wasn't here tonight at all. Longarm had no way of knowing when, or even if, the gunman would show up. All he could do at the moment was wait.

A short, stocky blonde in a low-cut, spangled blue dress

sidled up to him and said, "Hey, cowboy. My, you're a tall one, aren't you? And handsome, to boot."

Longarm smiled. "I appreciate the compliment, ma'am, but I ain't in the market tonight."

"Any man is in the market if the goods are tempting enough," she said. She stuck her chest out at him. "What do you think?"

He had to admit that her breasts were right attractive, what he could see of them, which was a lot. The deep valley between them had some freckles scattered in it. Somehow, they gave her an illusion of innocence that sort of balanced her obvious lack of same.

She wore too much war paint, but underneath it her face was still pretty. The thick curls piled on her head appeared to be a natural blond color. Longarm asked, "What's your name?"

"They call me Donna," she said, not exactly answering his question but close enough for government work or whoring.

"Well, Donna," he said, "you are a mighty attractive bit of business, and I don't mind sayin' so. But I'm still not in the market."

She pouted. "You could at least buy me a drink."

Longarm thought about it and nodded. "That I can do."

She called the bartender over and ordered whiskey. Longarm tossed a coin on the bar. He knew he was paying for watered-down tea but didn't care.

Donna picked up her drink and put her other hand on his chest. "If you change your mind, I'll be around."

Longarm's eyes were already roving over the crowd again. He nodded distractedly as he said, "All right."

He heard Donna's disgusted snort at his lack of interest. She turned to go find somebody else who might be interested in taking her upstairs. Longarm didn't figure she would be hurting for volunteers.

At that moment, a man pushed through the batwings at the main entrance and came into the saloon. It wasn't Joshua

Gullen, but Longarm knew instantly that the man was familiar to him. It took a second for the big lawman to remember where he had seen the newcomer.

It was the mustache, drooping like a pair of rat tails on
either side of the man's mouth, that made Longarm recall
him. He'd been at the market in La Villita when Longarm
was there the day before. In fact, he was the husband of the
woman who had told Longarm where to find old Gonzago.
It was entirely possible the skinny gent had overheard that
conversation, too.

But was he the one who had tipped off Gullen about
Longarm looking for the old man?

Thoughts whirled through Longarm's brain while he
watched the newcomer make his way over to one of the
tables where several men sat. Say somebody steals the Star
of Father Cristobal, he thought. The thief wants to know
what the writing on the back of the relic says, but even
though he spends days trying to figure it out, he can't get
the words to make any sense.

But he finds out somehow, maybe by asking around the
mission, that an old man called Gonzago claims to be able
to read the message, whatever it is. So he goes and kidnaps
Gonzago—or pays somebody to do it, more than likely—
and hires Gullen to keep an eye out for anybody else who
might be looking for the old man. This thief might even
have some spies working at the mission, Longarm mused.
The varmint could be staying one step ahead of him.

If the theory forming in Longarm's head was correct,
Gullen could have put out the word that he wanted to be
informed if anyone came around La Villita and started asking questions about Gonzago. The fella with the rat tail
mustache overhears the conversation between his wife and
a mysterious stranger who might be a lawman, so he goes
to see Gullen, who stakes out Gonzago's empty house . . .

It all added up, Longarm decided, and his ciphering was
usually right when it came to lawbreaking. All those thoughts
flashed through his mind in the time it took for Rat Tail to
walk over to that table and talk to the men sitting there. One

of them jerked a thumb toward the second floor.

Was he saying that Gullen was up there, Longarm wondered?

The man at the table shook his head. Rat Tail looked mad and said something else. Everybody was getting hot under the collar now, but one of the other men put out a hand in a calming gesture. He got to his feet, said something to Rat Tail, and then both of them started toward the stairs.

Those were some of Gullen's hired guns, Longarm thought, and one of them was taking Rat Tail upstairs to talk to Gullen himself.

Mere moments had passed since Donna gave up on him and started to walk off. Longarm turned his head quickly and saw that she had not gone far. She was already trying to hook another fish, though, as she insinuated herself mighty close to a man farther along the bar.

Longarm took a step and put a hand on her shoulder, interrupting the conversation. "Still want to go upstairs?" he asked Donna as she turned her head to look at him.

"Hey!" the man she was talking to protested. "You got a lot of nerve, mister!"

Longarm fixed him with a cold, level stare and said, "That's right. You want to find out how much?"

The man backed down immediately, holding up his hands and saying, "Forget it. I'm not gonna get myself killed over a whore. There's plenty more where she came from."

"But none as good as me," Donna said with a breathy laugh as she pressed her breasts against the big lawman's arm. "Once you make up your mind, you don't waste any time, do you, cowboy?"

"Nope," Longarm said as he grabbed her hand. "I want to get you upstairs right now!"

Chapter 8

There was nothing unusual about a big cowboy practically dragging one of the saloon girls toward the stairs. A fella could get mighty lonely riding the range.

So nobody in the Golden Dove paid much attention to Longarm as he led Donna across the room. The other men Rat Tail had accosted had gone back to their drinking and talking and didn't even glance toward the big lawman as he and Donna went past the table.

Longarm took the stairs two at a time. Donna had to hurry to keep up. She wasn't laughing now. She was starting to get irritated, in fact. She said, "Damn it, you don't have to be quite so enthusiastic, mister! It'll still be there when you get upstairs."

"I just can't wait to get a taste of you, honey," Longarm said to keep her cooperative.

She went back to simpering as they reached the second floor landing. "I'm gonna show you a really good time," she said. "In fact, if your thing ain't too big, I'll even let you stick it up my butt without charging you extra. I like it that way."

Longarm wasn't sure she would make that offer if she ever saw how he was built, which in all likelihood she probably never would. Because now that they had reached the top of the stairs, he saw a door swinging closed down at the end of the hall and figured that was where the gun-hand had taken Rat Tail.

"Where's your room?" he asked Donna.

"Right over here, sweetie." She tugged him toward one of the closed doors, on the opposite side of the hall from the room Longarm was interested in.

Well, having her take him to the room right next to that one would have been too much luck to expect, he thought briefly. He'd have to continue improvising.

She opened the door and led him inside the little room. The only furnishings were a bed, a ladderback chair, and a washstand. Donna closed the door, then turned her back to him and said, "You just get your duds off, honey, while I get ready."

For her, getting ready consisted of reaching down, grasping the hem of her short, spangled dress, and peeling it and her petticoat up and over her head, leaving her naked except for her button-up shoes and black stockings rolled down over her white thighs. Her ass was wide but very nicely rounded.

She looked surprised as she turned back to Longarm and saw that he was still completely dressed.

"Sweetie, you've got to take your clothes off before we can—" she began.

He hit her.

Longarm had been raised to be a gentleman. He had a chivalrous streak a mile wide in him. So it pained him greatly to strike a woman. But under the circumstances he didn't have much choice. He bunched his fist loosely and pulled his punch so he wouldn't hurt her too much, but he clipped her good enough that her eyes rolled up in their sockets and she dropped onto the narrow bed, out cold.

Quickly, he tore some strips off her petticoat and bound her hand and foot, then gagged her with another piece of cloth he tore from the garment. He shook his head in regret as he took a double eagle from his pocket and slapped it on the washstand.

He didn't want to think about what Henry would say if he wrote on his expense account: "$20 for tying and gagging a whore."

Donna would probably be happy when she woke up and saw the money, though. For twenty bucks, she probably would have let him do all that and more and squealed like she was enjoying it, to boot. Problem was, he didn't have time to explain what he was really after.

He slipped into the dimly lit hallway and cat-footed toward the door he had seen closing a few moments earlier. He didn't think Rat Tail had had time to conduct whatever business he was here for and then leave, so he ought to still be in there.

Sure enough, when Longarm pressed his ear to the panel, he heard men's voices talking animatedly inside. He couldn't make out all the words, but he thought he heard somebody say something in a whining tone about Gonzago and being promised something.

That would be Rat Tail. Gullen must have promised to pay for information about anybody looking for the old man, and then after Rat Tail had given him the tip on Longarm, Gullen had either shorted him on the money or reneged on the payoff completely. And now Rat Tail had gathered up his courage to come complain about it.

When the other man replied, his voice was too low for Longarm to understand anything he said. Grimacing in frustration, Longarm weighed his options.

He could kick the door down and charge into the room with his revolver in his hand, but there were at least two cold-blooded killers in there and the chances that gunplay would break out were mighty damn high. Longarm might be forced to kill Joshua Gullen and the other gunman before he could find out anything from them. Even worse, he might get drilled his ownself.

Or, he thought as he glanced around the corridor and his eye fell on a window at the end of it, there might be another way.

Keeping an eye on the door, he went quickly to the window and tested it to see how quietly he could raise it. The glass went up without making much racket. He had to hurry, because there was no telling when a customer from downstairs might bring one of the other whores up here for a roll in the hay.

He leaned out to take a look. There was a window in the wall a few feet away that would open into the room occupied by Gullen. Beyond that window was a door and the landing of an outside stairway that led down to the alley below.

It made sense that a man like Gullen, who was bound to have plenty of enemies, would want a way in and out where he wouldn't have to go through the saloon's crowded main room below.

Longarm gauged the distances and judged that the landing was too far away for him to jump for it. Instead he swung a leg over the windowsill, levered himself out, and hung from his hands for a second before dropping to the alley floor. He landed as lightly as he could and hoped it hadn't made too much of a thump. The window into Gullen's room was open several inches for ventilation.

Nobody came to the window to look out and yell. He hurried to the stairs and started up them, staying close to the wall so the boards would be less likely to squeak. When he reached the landing he slid silently over as close to the window as he could.

"—tired of arguing," a man was saying. "Give this greaser what he's got comin' to him, Luther."

"Sure, Joshua," another man said. That would be the gunnie who had brought Rat Tail up here.

Longarm suddenly had a bad feeling that Brother Rat Tail had bitten off too big a chunk of trouble for him to chew. That hunch was confirmed a second later when the skinny gent cried out in fear, "*Dios mio*, no!" There were the sounds of a brief struggle, an ugly gurgling noise, and a few seconds of a drumming sound that Longarm figured were the heels of Rat Tail's shoes beating out a last tattoo on the floor as he died.

The man's wife would have to run their stall at the market by herself from now on, Longarm supposed. He felt a moment's sympathy for her loss, even though her husband had been a greedy little, well, rat.

"What do you want me to do with him now that he's dead, Josh?" Luther asked.

"Take him out the back way and toss him in the river," Gullen replied. "Nobody'll pay any attention to one more dead Mex."

Longarm heard the hired killer moving around.

"What are you gonna do?"

"I thought I'd get Shifflet and go find that black-haired dancer from the cantina."

Longarm stiffened at those words.

"She's got to be the one who helped that bastard get away. It wasn't a coincidence those damn brothers of hers got in our way and slowed us down when we were trying to go after them."

Mercedes, Longarm thought. Gullen was smarter than he'd given the man credit for.

"It won't be hard to make her talk," Gullen went on. "She'll tell me who he is and where I can find him."

With a whisper of steel on leather, Longarm slipped his Colt from its holster. Gullen would never have a chance to hurt Mercedes. Longarm was about to kick down the door and go in shooting if he had to, when Luther asked, "What about the old man?"

That made Longarm pause and wait for Gullen's answer.

"What about him?" the hired killer snapped. "We did our job. We grabbed him and turned him over to that French fella who hired us. None of our business what happens to him after that. Our orders were just to get rid of anybody who showed up on their trail."

"I know, but I can't help but be curious about what's so damn important about some old greaser."

"I don't know and I don't care. Now get that body out of here. Good idea, choking him to death, by the way. Didn't get any blood on the floor that way."

"Yeah, but it looks like he pissed and shit himself when he died."

"Son of a—! Just clean up that mess and get him out of here."

Footsteps came toward the door. Longarm backed off a little, holding the Colt level at his waist. Luther was going to have a hell of a surprise waiting for him when he stepped out onto the landing.

But Longarm had an even bigger surprise coming. Down below in the alley, a man suddenly yelled, "Somebody's up there on the landing outside the boss's room! Shoot the son of a bitch!"

Chapter 9

Gun thunder filled the alley as garish muzzle flashes ripped through the darkness. The men down below didn't know who was up on the landing and didn't care. All they knew was that someone was skulking around the door of Gullen's room, and their first impulse was to kill.

Bullets chewed splinters from the railing around the landing, thudded into the wall, and whistled around Longarm's head. He twisted away from the onslaught, but there was nowhere for him to go.

Except through the door.

Longarm rammed his shoulder against the panel. The flimsy lock gave way and the jamb splintered under the impact. The door flew open. Longarm fell through it, his momentum taking him to one knee.

As the big lawman surged to his feet again, he saw a stunned-looking Luther, the man who had brought Rat Tail up here, standing only a couple of feet away. The gunnie must have realized that he ought to do something about this unexpected intruder, because he abruptly clawed at the gun on his hip.

Longarm grabbed the man's collar with his free hand and flung him toward the doorway. As he staggered out onto the landing, unable to stop himself, Luther only had time to yell, "Don't shoot, boys, it's—" before several shots triggered from the alley ripped through his body. Screaming, he hit the flimsy railing and burst through it to plummet to the ground.

Inside the room, Longarm had to dive for the floor as Gullen fired at him from behind a desk where the hired killer had ducked to take cover. The slug racketed over Longarm's head. Longarm caught a glimpse under the desk of one of Gullen's booted feet. He threw a snap shot at it, hoping to cripple the gunman, but all he succeeded in doing was blowing the heel off Gullen's boot.

That made Gullen yelp in pain anyway and lose his balance as he crouched behind the desk. As he started to fall, he swept his arm across the desk, sending the lamp that sat there flying toward Longarm. He rolled away from it as it hit the floor and shattered.

Kerosene spilled from the broken reservoir and went up in a sudden sheet of flame between Longarm and Gullen. Both men fired their guns through it. Longarm couldn't tell if he hit Gullen or not. Gullen seemed plenty spry as he leaped for the door to the corridor and slapped it open, though. Longarm triggered again, but Gullen disappeared, never slowing down.

Footsteps pounded on the outside stairs. A man yelled, "Josh! Josh! Are you all right?"

One of the gunnies appeared in the doorway and spotted Longarm. His gun swung up.

Longarm was on the floor next to Rat Tail's corpse. He grabbed the back of the dead man's shirt and hauled him upright. The gunman's bullet thudded into Rat Tail's body. Longarm shoved his Colt under the corpse's arm and fired, blowing the man back out through the door.

Somebody yelled, "Let's get the hell out of here!" Boot leather smacked the steps, going down this time. Gullen's men had just run out of loyalty to their boss.

Longarm shoved the corpse aside and got to his feet. Heat from the flames beat at his face, and his shirt was smoldering in a couple of places.

He wanted to go after Gullen, but at the same time, the fire was nearly out of control. If the flames reached the walls, this old frame building would go up like a tinderbox. He holstered his gun, snatched the rug from the floor, and started beating at the fire.

Donna was probably still tied up in the room down the hall. She would die if the fire raged out of control, and there was no telling how many others would lose their lives as well. No matter how much Longarm wanted to go after Gullen, no matter how worried he was about Mercedes, he couldn't ignore that danger.

The shooting and the smoke had caused quite a commotion. People were yelling downstairs and in some of the other rooms up here. As Longarm slapped out the last of the flames with the charred rug, a couple of men he recognized as bartenders tried to crowd through the doorway. He knew if he tried to go out that way, it would take him a long time to push through the mob, time he probably couldn't afford to waste.

He turned and lunged for the outside stairs instead.

Men shouted for him to stop, but nobody fired any shots or came after him. He bounded down the stairs, taking them three at a time.

He had to get to La Villita as fast as he could. Mercedes would probably be at the cantina by now, dancing as she always did. Gullen couldn't grab her and threaten her right there in the middle of the place, but he could wait for her to leave and get her then.

Longarm intended to be there well before that could happen.

He raced to the livery stable and threw his saddle on the rented horse, much to the consternation of the surprised hostler. Galloping out of the barn, he headed for the cantina.

As he rode, he thought about what he had overheard through that open window before all hell broke loose. The theory he had put together earlier in his mind seemed to be right. Somebody had paid Gullen to kidnap old Gonzago and cover up the trail. Gullen had delivered the old man to his mysterious employer, who was evidently a Frenchman.

But who was the man, and where could he be found? Longarm didn't have the answers to those questions, but Gullen could give them to him.

A few minutes later, Longarm swung down from the saddle outside the cantina. He heard music coming from inside . . . the music of a couple of twin guitars.

Relief went through him. If her brothers were playing, Mercedes had to be dancing.

But as he stepped through the beaded doorway and looked around, he saw no flashing brown legs, no tossing mane of midnight black hair. The brothers, Eduardo and Jaime, were playing, all right, but the open space where Mercedes danced was empty.

Longarm didn't see Joshua Gullen anywhere inside the cantina, either.

Cold fear replaced the relief he had felt a moment earlier. Everything seemed perfectly normal inside the cantina except for Mercedes' absence.

The brothers saw him coming but continued playing until Longarm reached out and closed his hand around the neck of one of the guitars, stilling the strings. Whichever brother owned the instrument he had silenced let out a curse. The other one stopped playing as well, and one of his hands strayed toward a knife tucked behind his belt.

"Take it easy, old son," Longarm said. "Just tell me where your sister is tonight."

"You should leave her alone," the young man said angrily. "You bring her nothing but trouble. Because of you, she is hurt."

"You mean her arm?"

"*Sí.* It was sore tonight, so she decided not to dance."

"So she's home?" Longarm asked. His jaw clenched tightly with worry.

"*Sí,* of course. Where else would she be?"

In a low, deadly voice, Longarm asked, "Has Joshua Gullen been here?"

The brothers exchanged a glance, then one of them nodded and said, "He came in a few minutes ago but left as soon as he looked around."

Longarm bit back a curse. He knew what Gullen's actions meant. When the hired killer had seen that Mercedes wasn't here, he must have assumed that she was at home. That's where he would go next to look for her.

By now everyone in the cantina was watching the confrontation with rapt attention. Longarm let go of the guitar and turned to hurry out of the place, ignoring their watching eyes.

He had hold of his horse's reins before he realized he wasn't exactly sure he knew how to get to Mercedes' house from the cantina. He left the horse there and started retracing their escape route from the night before in his mind and on foot. When he was finally sure of his landmarks, he broke into a run.

He turned onto the narrow street where Mercedes lived. The people who were out and about in La Villita tonight must have wondered why this tall gringo was running around like a madman.

As he approached her house, he saw the warm glow of lamplight through a window. No horse was tied outside. Maybe Gullen hadn't gotten here yet, Longarm told himself. Maybe.

He didn't stop to knock on the door, just jerked it open and called, "Mercedes! Mercedes, are you here?"

A low moan was the only answer.

Lips pulling back from his teeth, Longarm rushed through the small front room toward the even smaller bedroom. A familiar coppery scent hit his nostrils and turned his spine to ice. The light from the other room fell across a crumpled figure on the floor beside the bed.

Longarm dropped to his knees beside her, pulled her up and into his lap. She wore the same sort of long skirt and white blouse she had worn in the cantina the night before, but the middle of the blouse was dark and sodden with the freshly spilled blood he had smelled when he came in.

That wasn't the only wound she had. Somebody had taken a knife to her face as well.

"Damn it, no!" Longarm breathed. "Mercedes!"

Her eyes fluttered open. He saw the ragged beat of her pulse jumping in her throat.

"Custis . . ." she whispered. Her voice was as fragile and gossamer as a butterfly's wing.

"Gullen did this," he said between gritted teeth.

It wasn't a question, but she said, "*Sí*. He and another man . . . hurt me . . . made me tell him . . . made me tell him about you . . . how you are a marshal . . . I am . . . so sorry, Custis."

"Never you mind about that," he told her as he cradled her against him. "Don't you worry about it for a second."

"I was brave . . . as long as I could be . . ."

"I know," he said. "I know."

"And then . . . and then since I knew . . . he was going to kill me anyway . . . I fought him . . . I got the knife . . . I cut *him* . . ."

"Good for you, darlin'," Longarm whispered as he tightened his arms around her. "Good for you."

"But he took it away from me . . . stabbed me . . . he thought I was dead." One of her bloodstained hands came up and caught at his arm with unexpected strength. She raised her head and turned it to look at him. Somehow she was summoning up the last of her willpower in order to do this as she said again, "Custis, he thought I was dead. He was talking to the other man . . . He said something about the Star of Father Cristobal . . . how it must be worth . . . even more than he thought . . . and the old man, too . . . He said a name . . . Rostand . . . at the Menger . . ."

Rostand? Gullen's mysterious employer? Had to be, Longarm thought. If this fella Rostand could afford to stay at the Menger, he could probably afford to hire a kidnapper and killer like Gullen.

Who, from the sound of the things that Mercedes had overheard while Gullen thought she was already dead, Gullen was thinking about double-crossing, or at least horning in on whatever game Rostand was playing.

The part of Longarm's brain that was a lawman's brain put those clues together in a hurry, making the connections guided by instinct and long experience.

The part of him that had liked Mercedes one hell of a lot, that had been grateful to her for her help, that had thoroughly enjoyed the time he had spent with her . . . that part was plunged into an icy bath of grief and rage. The only thing this beautiful young woman had done was save his life, and for that she had been tortured and murdered.

Joshua Gullen would pay for what he had done, even if Longarm had to track him to the ends of the earth. Longarm made that vow to himself.

"Do you hear . . . the music?" Mercedes suddenly asked in an even fainter whisper than before.

Longarm leaned closer to her face. "Music?"

"My brothers . . . they play their guitars . . . so fast, so sweet . . . do you hear it, Custis?"

"I hear it," Longarm told her, forcing out the words.

"It makes me want to dance . . ."

"Go ahead and dance, Mercedes. Dance to the music."

Her hands lifted. Her head went back. She said, "Ahhhh . . ." in a long sigh that ended with her limp and lifeless in Longarm's embrace. He sat there and held her and watched the flame flicker in the lamp on the table in the front room.

"You don't know it yet, Gullen," he said to the quiet room, "but you're a dead man, old son."

Chapter 10

Longarm hated to leave Mercedes' body there for her brothers to find later, but he still had a job to do. He lifted her onto the bed and covered her. His hands were red with her blood and so was his shirt. There was nothing he could do about that.

When he got back to the cantina, the rented horse shied nervously at the smell of blood on him. "Take it easy, you jughead," he said as he jerked the reins loose from the hitch rail. He mounted up and rode toward downtown.

He couldn't walk into a fancy place like the Menger Hotel looking like he had just come from a slaughterhouse. Folks would start yelling for the law. Even if he pulled out his badge and showed them that he worked for Uncle Sam, it would still slow things down and be a needless complication.

So when he got back to the livery stable, he rousted out the elderly hostler, who stared at the gory apparition confronting him like Longarm was a ghost or something.

"I need to get cleaned up," Longarm told him. "You got a clean shirt around here?"

"Nothin' that'll fit a big galoot like you, mister," the hostler said.

Longarm slapped a double eagle into the man's trembling hand. "Then go find a general store that's open and buy me one," he ordered. "Make it fast, too."

"Mister, I . . . I don't want to get mixed up in no trouble . . ."

"You won't be," Longarm promised. "I'm a deputy U.S. marshal. Now go!"

The hostler went.

By the time he got back ten minutes later carrying a new shirt that Longarm hoped would at least come close to fitting, the big lawman had gone out back to the pump and scrubbed off as much of Mercedes' blood as he could. He tossed his ruined shirt into a rubbish barrel.

As he pulled on the new one, he nodded to the hostler. "I'm obliged for your help, old-timer. You keep the change from that gold piece."

The hostler swallowed hard. "All right, but . . . mister, are you a madman?"

"I'm mad, all right," Longarm said, thinking of how he would avenge Mercedes' murder, no matter what it took. "But I ain't loco."

Obviously, the hostler didn't believe that. He looked relieved to have escaped with his own life as Longarm left the livery stable and headed for the Menger Hotel a few blocks away.

He tied the horse outside the hotel, which had several entrances. He used the one that went directly into the hotel's bar. With slitted eyes, he studied the men in the place but didn't see Gullen. He didn't know what the man with Gullen looked like. Shifflet, that was the hombre's name, Longarm recalled.

Shifflet had helped torture and kill Mercedes, so he was doomed and damned, too, as far as Longarm was concerned. First things first, though. He went through the bar and into the lobby. A quick look around told him that Gullen wasn't here, either.

He went up to the fancy counter where a clerk was working. "M'sieu Rostand, please," he said, using the French term as if it came naturally to him.

The clerk shook his head. "I'm sorry, sir. Mr. Rostand and his sister checked out a few minutes ago."

This was the first Longarm had heard about a sister, but it had only been an hour or so since he'd first heard of Rostand. There was still a lot that he didn't know.

"They checked out at this time of night?"

"Our guests come and go on *their* schedule, sir, not ours," the clerk told him with a faint sneer.

Longarm reined in the impulse to push that sneer down the hombre's throat with his fist. "Do you happen to know where they were goin' from here?"

"As a matter of fact, Mr. Rostand asked me about the best way to get to get to Corpus Christi." The clerk's eyes narrowed suspiciously. "Are you a friend of theirs? You don't exactly look like the sort of man who would make their acquaintance."

"Never you mind about that," Longarm snapped. "There's no train to Corpus. What about a stagecoach?"

"I think I've answered quite enough of your questions. If you have no further business here, I'm afraid I'll have to ask you to leave." The clerk's tone made it clear that he thought Longarm was cluttering up the Menger's lobby.

That was enough to fray Longarm's last nerve. He reached across the counter, grabbed the clerk's frilly shirt, and jerked the fella toward him before the clerk knew what was going on. Putting his face close to the clerk's suddenly frightened features, Longarm grated, "Tell me how they were gonna get to Corpus Christi."

Before the clerk could answer, a man's voice behind Longarm said loudly and harshly, "Let go of him, mister, or you'll regret it!"

Longarm didn't release the clerk right away. Instead he looked back over his shoulder and saw a big man wearing the gray uniform and shield of the San Antonio police force. The town still had a city marshal, Longarm knew, but in recent years instead of deputies, the marshal oversaw a regular uniformed force like in the bigger cities back East.

This policeman was backing up the order he'd given

with a gun in his hand, pointed at Longarm. "Take it easy," Longarm said. "I ain't gonna hurt the fella."

He let go of the clerk, who reeled back breathless with fear. Longarm turned toward the policeman, who snapped, "Keep your hand away from that gun. I'll shoot if I have to."

Longarm shook his head and began, "We're on the same side—"

"Are you the gent who came into a livery stable not far from here covered with blood a few minutes ago?" the officer demanded. "And before you bother denying it, I'll tell you that I don't mind marching you back down there so the hostler can identify you."

Obviously the hostler had gotten worried enough to go and find a lawman. Longarm sighed and kept a tight rein on his impatience and anger. While he was having to deal with this, Rostand and his sister were getting away, and so were Gullen and Shifflet.

"Yeah, I had blood on my shirt," he admitted.

The policeman's eyes narrowed in his broad, ruddy face. "You know, you match the description of the fella who assaulted a, uh, lady of the evening at the Golden Dove earlier tonight. Right before there was a fire and a bunch of shooting and some dead men scattered around. You better come with me. Take that gun out, slow and easy, and put it on the counter."

"Listen to me," Longarm said. "I'm a U.S. deputy marshal. If you promise not to get trigger-happy, I'll show you my badge and bona fides."

"You can show 'em to my boss down at the Bat Cave."

From previous visits to San Antonio, Longarm recalled that the so-called Bat Cave was actually the brick building that housed the city jail and the headquarters of the police force. Maybe it was time to stop playing a lone hand and take advantage of the help he might be able to get from the local authorities.

"All right," he said. Slowly and carefully, he used his left hand to ease the .44 from its holster and placed it on the counter. The scared clerk looked at the gun like it was a diamondback rattlesnake and edged farther away from it. Longarm kept his hands in plain sight and stepped to the side. The gray-uniformed officer moved in and scooped up the Colt.

"Get movin'," he growled. "And if you try anything funny, I'll bust your head open."

As he thought about Mercedes, Longarm said, "I can promise you, old son . . . right now the last thing I'm feelin' is funny."

Longarm didn't know if City Marshal Phil Shardein had already gone to bed when he was summoned to the Bat Cave, but Shardein had the grumpy, impatient look of a man who had been roused from sleep. The local lawman tossed the leather folder containing Longarm's badge and identification papers onto his desk and glared at him.

"Usually when an out-of-town star packer comes into my jurisdiction, he lets me know about it," Shardein said.

"I meant to, Marshal," Longarm said. "I just sort of hadn't gotten around to it."

Shardein grunted. "Did you mean to report all the shootings and killings you've been mixed up in since you've been here, too? Or were you just not getting around to that?" One of the marshal's big hands slapped down on the desk. "My God, man, massacres have just been following you around!"

Longarm had to admire the San Antonio police force's ability to gather and coordinate information. In less than an hour's time, Shardein had reports on his desk concerning the ruckus at the cantina last night, the melee at the Golden Dove, Longarm's confrontation with Mercedes' brothers tonight, and the discovery of her body at her house.

The one thing all that had in common was Longarm himself, so he couldn't blame Shardein for being suspicious. Probably the only reason Longarm wasn't locked up in one of the Bat Cave's cells was that he had convinced Shardein to send a wire to Billy Vail to confirm his identity and his reason for being in San Antonio.

Luckily, Vail had answered quickly, although he probably

wasn't happy about his top deputy getting himself arrested like this.

"Are you lettin' me go?" Longarm asked.

"I shouldn't. I ought to stick you in a cell and leave you there overnight to cool off." The city marshal shrugged. "But according to Chief Marshal Vail, you're on the up-and-up and reasonably honest, so I guess I believe you when you say all those killings were either self-defense or committed by someone else. Now tell me about the Star of Father Cristobal."

"I expect you got a report about the relic bein' stolen?"

Shardein shuffled through some of the papers on his desk and nodded. "I did. According to this, though, there really wasn't anything we could do about it. There were no clues, no indication of who might have taken it."

"I can tell you that. Joshua Gullen took it, or somebody else hired by this fella Rostand."

"Yeah, you said that already." Shardein consulted another piece of paper. "According to the records at the Menger, the man's name is Maurice Rostand. He's been staying there for the past two weeks, along with his sister, Jeanne. Why would Rostand pay somebody to steal some old religious relic?"

Longarm shook his head. "Now, that I don't know. But I'm sure he's behind it. I heard Gullen say that Rostand paid him to kidnap old Gonzago, who claimed to be able to read the writing on the back of the Star, so it has to have something to do with that."

Shardein frowned and said, "Rostand's been here for two weeks. Why would he cut and run tonight?"

"Because he found out there's a federal lawman on the trail of the Star and old Gonzago. I reckon he or Gullen paid off one of the servants at the mission to let 'em know if anybody other than the local badge toters showed up asking about the Star. My visit with Father Tomás would have made them suspicious yesterday, and then when Gullen got another tip that I was interested in Gonzago, too, he knew he had to get rid of me, even though he didn't know who I am. That's why he bushwhacked me last night and tried to find me today. I found him first, though. But he got away from me and tortured that poor girl Mercedes into tellin' him that I'm a deputy U.S. marshal." Longarm raked a thumbnail along his jaw. "I figure Gullen was already gettin' a mite greedy before that. He wanted to horn in on whatever Rostand's game is, instead of just bein' a hired gun for him. So when he found out who I am, he came here and told Rostand, on the condition that Rostand take him in as a partner. The idea that federal law was on his trail spooked Rostand enough so he gathered up his sister and took off for the tall and uncut, probably with Gullen and Shifflet taggin' along."

Shardein glared at him again. "You can't prove a damn bit of that."

"No," Longarm admitted, "but it makes sense. Maybe I've got a little detail wrong here and there, but I'd bet a hat most of it's right."

"I'm still not clear why the federal government is interested in all this."

"Because somebody in Washington got the idea that it might upset relations between us and whoever's in charge down there in Mexico City this week. It was still Presidente Diaz, last time I heard, but you can't ever tell about that place. They have revolutions like we have church socials. As for me . . ." Longarm shrugged. "I'm after the Star and Rostand and Gullen because it's my job."

And because this mess had gotten a fine young woman killed and her death had to be avenged, he added to himself.

"So what are you going to do now?" Shardein wanted to know.

"You said there's no stagecoach that leaves in the middle of the night for Corpus Christi."

"That's right. The next coach out of here bound for Corpus is at nine o'clock tomorrow morning. I had a man go and check with the stagecoach office to be sure about that."

"And there's no train that goes down there yet. So if Rostand and his sister left San Antonio tonight, they did it on horseback or in a private vehicle."

Shardein shook his head. "I can't see a fella like Rostand, who's supposed to be rich, riding horseback all the way to Corpus."

"Neither can I," Longarm agreed. "Can you have your men ask around at the livery stables and try to find out if anybody rented a buggy or a carriage to a Frenchman and his sister tonight?"

Shardein thought about the request and after a moment gave a grudging nod. "I suppose I can do that."

Longarm got to his feet. "Then if you ain't gonna throw me in the hoosegow—you ain't, are you?"

Shardein frowned and said, "I suppose not . . . although there's a big part of me that sure wants to."

"Then I'm gonna head back to my hotel and get some sleep. I'll start out on their trail in the morning. Maybe by then I'll know what sort of vehicle they're using. That'll make it easier to track them."

"Corpus is way out of my jurisdiction," Shardein mused. "I suppose since you pack a star for Uncle Sam, you don't have to worry about such things. You can go anywhere you want as long as you don't leave the country."

"That's right," Longarm said.

Anywhere in the country . . . and anywhere else he had to go in order to track down Gullen and Rostand, find out what this was all about, and deliver justice. To the ends of the earth, he had promised himself as he held Mercedes while she died.

And he meant it.

Chapter 11

The next morning, Longarm rode south from San Antonio on a different horse. The one he'd been using was fine for town work, but since he had a ways to go and didn't know when he'd be back, he had paid a visit to Fort Sam Houston and picked up an army mount. A big, strong roan gelding, it wasn't much on looks but he could tell it had plenty of stamina. The animal ought to hold up fine during the several days it would take him to reach the seaport town of Corpus Christi.

Early that morning, one of Marshal Shardein's men had knocked on the door of Longarm's hotel room and handed the big lawman a report stating that a man matching Maurice Rostand's description had picked up a carriage and a four-horse team from a wagon yard the previous evening. Rostand hadn't just rented the vehicle and the team. He had *bought* them, paying cash. The owner of the wagon yard had been glad to get out of bed in order to conduct the transaction, since Rostand hadn't haggled but had paid the asking price.

The police had also found a porter at the Menger Hotel who had loaded the bags belonging to M'sieu Rostand and his sister onto the carriage a short time after that. According to the man's story, Rostand and his sister had ridden off in

the carriage while a rough-looking man handled the reins
and another man accompanied them on horseback. The
rider was ugly and dangerous-looking, with a lantern jaw
and a fresh cut on his face.

When Longarm read that, he remembered what Mercedes had told him about getting her hands on the knife and
doing some damage to Gullen. *Good for you, darlin',* he
thought.

Armed with that information, Longarm had checked out
of his hotel, picked up the army mount, and headed south.

He didn't have any idea where Rostand had been keeping Gonzago. Obviously, he wasn't holding the old man
prisoner in the Menger but had had him stashed somewhere
else. Rostand had probably picked him up on the way out
of town the night before.

Unless the Frenchman had already forced Gonzago to
translate the writing on the back of the Star of Father Cristobal, which was a distinct possibility. If that were the case,
old Gonzago was probably already dead.

That thought put a bleak expression on Longarm's face.
He hoped Gonzago was smart enough to know that the
mysterious writing on the back of the artifact was the only
thing keeping him alive.

Longarm heeled the roan into a ground-eating lope. His
hope was that he could move at a faster pace than the carriage in which Maurice and Jeanne Rostand rode. His hope
was that he could catch up to them before they reached
Corpus Christi. The first thought that had come to him
when he heard where they were headed was that they intended to board a ship at the port city and sail away.

If that happened, he was going to have a hell of a lot
harder time finding them. Things would sure be simpler if
he could nab them while they were still on American soil.

The terrain between San Antonio and the coast consisted
of rolling plains with nothing to slow a man down. Longarm covered a lot of ground that first day. He stopped at a
couple of roadside taverns along the way to find out if anyone had seen the Rostand carriage go by. If he was really

lucky, the travelers might have even stopped at one of the same places and inadvertently revealed more about their plans.

He wasn't *that* fortunate, but at the second tavern, one of the loafers sitting on a stool outside recalled seeing a fancy carriage go by around midday.

Longarm's quarry was still several hours ahead of him, but he was convinced he had cut into the lead.

He rode until nearly dark and stopped for the night in a tiny settlement where there was no hotel. The fella who owned a blacksmith shop and stable let him sleep in the hayloft for a dollar, though, and threw in water and grain for Longarm's horse as well. Longarm ate supper at the local saloon, the first meal he'd had since breakfast early that morning in San Antonio. Talking to the customers in the saloon didn't produce any more information about the people he sought. They must have driven right on through without stopping.

The next day was more of the same: heat, monotonous country, dusty little settlements that weren't much more than wide places in the road. In one of them, though, he received confirmation that he was still on the right trail.

"Yeah, they was here, all right," said a grizzled, middle-aged man who was the owner of a big, weathered frame building that served as hotel, saloon, and general store for the surrounding area. I don't think the two furriners liked it much, but where else was they gonna stay, out here on the middle o' nowhere?"

"They were travelin' in a fancy carriage?"

The man nodded. "That's right. Fine-lookin' team pullin' it, too."

"What'd they look like?" Longarm hadn't seen Maurice and Jeanne Rostand, but he had their descriptions.

"Oh, I don't know about the fella. He was just average, I reckon. Dark hair. Kind of slick-lookin'. The gal, though . . ." The proprietor let out an admiring whistle. "She was a real looker, though, lemme tell you. Had that dark red hair and pale skin. Nice bustle, too. The fella said she was his sister.

I didn't really believe him at first. But he got two rooms, so I reckon maybe he was tellin' the truth." The man lowered his voice. "Although I figured with him bein' a Frenchman and all, he'd fuck anybody, even his own sister. They didn't, though."

Longarm didn't ask the man how he knew that. Probably spent the night with his ear pressed against Jeanne Rostand's door, the dirty-minded old so-and-so.

"Were there two men traveling with them?"

"Three," the man said. "Ugly-lookin' fella who looked like he'd been in a knife fight a day or two ago, a big hombre with a beard, and an old man. The old-timer was sick, if you ask me. He was sure worried-lookin'."

Longarm kept his face impassive, even though he felt a surge of excitement. For the first time, he had proof that old Gonzago was still alive, or at least had been the night before.

"Did the old man say anything?"

The proprietor shook his head. "No, the furrin fella did the talkin' for all of them. He got three rooms. One for him, one for his sis, and one for the other fellas. Didn't hardly seem fair, makin' the three of them share one room, but that's the way them snooty furriners are, I guess. They don't care all that much if the folks workin' for 'em are comfortable."

"They stayed the night and then left this morning?"

"Yep. I fed 'em breakfast before they left. The man and his sis just sort of picked at it. Guess it weren't to their taste. I can't cook nothin' but good ol' American food, though. Them Frenchies don't like it, it's too damn bad."

"So they headed for Corpus Christi, did they?"

"No, sir. Took the Rockport road when they left."

That surprised Longarm. Everything so far had pointed toward Corpus.

"Are you sure about that?" he asked.

"Yeah. Seen it with my own eyes. The turn-off's only a couple hundred yards down the road. I was watchin' when they swung that direction." The man sighed. "You sure don't see a gal that pretty around these parts too often. She can come back here anytime she wants."

Longarm thought it was extremely unlikely Jeanne Rostand would ever set foot in this squalid little settlement again, but he didn't see any point in saying that. He thanked the proprietor for his help, mounted up, and rode slowly down the road toward the Rockport cut-off.

The wheels in Longarm's brain were turning over again. Rostand had known that he was still alive and still represented a possible threat to whatever plans the man had. So asking the clerk at the Menger about the best way to get to Corpus Christi could have been a ploy intended to send Longarm down the wrong road. And it probably would have worked, too, if Jeanne Rostand's beauty hadn't made that lecherous hotel man stare after the carriage in unrequited longing as it departed.

Longarm's hunch about Rostand planning to get away on a boat could still be true. Rockport was about thirty miles up the coast from Corpus Christi. A couple of past assignments had taken Longarm there, so he was familiar with the place. It was mostly a fishing town now, but a decade earlier, a lot of South Texas cattle had been shipped out from there and the neighboring settlement of Fulton. As a result, the area still had a pretty rough reputation. Long barrier islands lay several miles offshore, but there were several cuts where seagoing vessels could come through. A ship that sailed from Rockport could get anywhere a ship that departed from Corpus Christi could.

Yeah, Rostand's question to the clerk had been a trick, Longarm decided. Rockport was their real destination.

And now it was his, he thought as he veered his mount onto the road that led southeast.

During his earlier trips to these parts, he had run into cannibal Indians and what was supposed to be a pirate's ghost. Longarm hoped nothing like that would happen this time. He just wanted to arrest Maurice Rostand, free old Gonzago, and kill Joshua Gullen. He supposed he would have to give Gullen a chance to surrender—as long as he was packing a badge, he couldn't just gun anybody down in cold blood, even a snake like Gullen—but he was confident that the hired killer wouldn't come peacefully. That would be just fine.

Longarm rode along Water Street with the gentle waves of the bay lapping at the shoreline to his right. To his left was a row of neat little cottages. Up ahead he saw the tall masts of ships in the harbor.

It was late afternoon. Rostand, Gullen, and the others could have boarded a ship and sailed by now, but Longarm thought there was a good chance they were still here. He had pushed the roan hard, and the horse had responded gallantly. He didn't think his quarry could have beaten him to Rockport by more than an hour or two.

He passed the row of cottages and entered a stretch of several blocks lined with businesses. If Rostand believed that they had succeeded in decoying him to Corpus Christi, would they go to the trouble to hide the carriage?

Longarm didn't know, but he figured it was a place to start looking.

He stopped at the first livery stable he came to. The man who ran the place looked at the roan with admiration, noted the US brand on its hip, and said, "Used to be an army mount, didn't it?"

"That's right," Longarm said. If the man wanted to assume that he had bought the horse from the army, Longarm wasn't going to disabuse him of the notion.

"I can tell by that McClellan saddle you used to be in the Union cavalry, too."

Longarm shrugged. It was his habit not to tell anyone which side he had supported in the Late Unpleasantness. Some folks were still fighting the war fifteen years after it was over. It was easier just to say that he disremembered.

"Don't worry, mister, nobody around here will give you any trouble for bein' a Yankee. This bein' a seaport town, we get folks from all over the world comin' and goin'. People tend to get along. Better for business that way."

Longarm nodded and said, "That's good to know." Since
the man had given him an opening, he took it. "As a matter
of fact, I'm lookin' for some friends of mine from France.
They were supposed to be gettin' to Rockport any day now.
Maybe you've seen 'em. They'll be travelin' in a nice carriage with a team of four fine-lookin' horses."

The liveryman shook his head. "Nope, I think I'd remember that. I got an eye for horseflesh, you might say. But
if they're well-to-do enough to have a carriage like that,
they're probably stayin' at the Austin House. Nicest hotel in
town."

"I'm obliged," Longarm said. "I'll ask up there. In the
meantime, you'll take care of this big fella for me?"

The man patted the roan's shoulder. "Sure. Be glad to."

Longarm paid for a couple of nights in advance and left
the livery stable. Water Street had turned into Austin Street,
and he saw the hotel up ahead, a big, sprawling frame structure with four stories and galleries all around on the bottom
two. The outside walls were whitewashed, and the roof was
painted a bright blue. Colorful flags fluttered from poles
attached to the roof gables. The hotel was set in a big green
lawn that sloped very gently down to a narrow strip of sand
along the water.

Longarm frowned as he paused in front of a barbershop
down the block and looked at the hotel. He couldn't just
waltz in there and ask to speak to Maurice Rostand . . . or
could he? The Austin House wasn't like that place where the
fugitives had stayed the night before. Rostand couldn't drag
a pair of hired guns and a scared old Mexican into a genteel
hostelry like this and not arouse considerable curiosity.

That meant there was a good chance Gullen and Shifflet
were holed up somewhere else, some place they could keep
Gonzago prisoner without anybody caring. So Gullen might
not be at the hotel to recognize him if he walked in.

Asking would sure be the quickest and easiest way to
find out if the Rostands were there, he decided. He didn't
want to confront them just yet, not until he had a little better grasp on the lay of the land.

Maybe it would be a good idea to clean up a mite first. If he walked into the Austin House looking like a grubline-riding cowboy, he might shock some of the folks staying there. He had left his saddle at the livery stable, but he was toting his Winchester and war bag. He carried them up one of the side streets until he found a boardinghouse that had a room to rent. The widow lady who ran the place was glad to take his money, even though he couldn't tell her for sure how long he would be staying.

The boardinghouse didn't have any bathing facilities, but he was able to wash up and shave and put on a clean shirt to go with his tweed suit. After he'd brushed the trail dust off his hat and boots, he judged that he looked halfway respectable. Enough so he probably wouldn't cause any high-toned ladies to faint at the sight of him in the Austin House lobby, anyway.

"Do you know if any ships sailed today?" he paused to ask the landlady on his way out of the boardinghouse.

"Passenger ships, you mean?"

"Yes'm."

The woman pursed her lips and shook her head. "I don't believe so, and I keep up with the arrivals and departures fairly well. My late husband worked at the harbor, so I always knew what was going on down there. I just got in the habit of keeping up with it, I guess. Of course, we don't actually get many passenger ships here. Mostly cargo vessels and fishing boats, a few private yachts and things like that."

Longarm's ears perked up at that. Was Maurice Rostand rich enough to have his own yacht meet him and his sister here? Based on what he had heard about the man so far, Longarm couldn't rule it out.

He gave a polite tug on his hat and said, "I'm obliged, ma'am," then left the boardinghouse and headed for the waterfront.

Dusk was coming on. The wind from offshore, which was a real howler sometimes, had laid down so that the pennants on the roof of the hotel flapped lazily back and forth. Despite the fact that the air was sticky as hell here along the coast, the sweltering heat that Longarm had felt inland didn't reach this far. As the evening came on, the weather was warm but pleasant. The sky was a mixture of thick clouds and fading blue.

The bottom floor of the hotel was set up about six feet in the air on thick pillars, in case the water got up during a hurricane. Longarm had been through a couple of those varmints, including the one that had blown away the town of Indianola, up the coast about sixty miles from here, and he didn't want to ever experience another one.

He went up a walk of crushed shells and climbed the stairs to the first floor gallery. Ladies in hats and big-bustled dresses strolled along the gallery accompanied by gents in straw boaters and high, tight collars. Longarm could practically smell the money in the air as he went into the lobby.

Crystal chandeliers hung from the ceiling, overstuffed armchairs and divans were scattered around, and potted palms stood in the corners. If not for the sea breeze blowing through from the open doors in the rear of the lobby, Longarm might have thought he was in some fancy hotel in Chicago.

He went to the desk on the left side of the room and gave a pleasant nod to the fair-haired clerk. Trying not to sound too much like the rough-around-the-edges frontiersman he really was, he said, "Pardon me, but do my friends the Rostands happen to be staying here?"

The clerk smiled at him. "You're in luck, sir," he said. "There's Mademoiselle Rostand now." He raised a hand to signal, ignoring the warning look in Longarm's widening eyes, and called, "Oh, Mademoiselle Rostand, there's a gentleman here who'd like to see you!"

Chapter 12

Longarm wanted to ask the hombre behind the desk if he was really as dumb as a sackful of rocks or just liked to act that way.

But there was no time for that now, no time for anything except turning around and plastering what he hoped wasn't a too phony-looking grin on his face.

He knew from the descriptions he'd heard that Jeanne Rostand was supposed to be an attractive woman, but he wasn't prepared for just how beautiful she really was.

She carried a parasol and wore a lightweight green gown that was high-necked and long-sleeved, but despite its conservative cut, it hugged her closely enough to reveal the finely curved lines of her body. Thick auburn hair was pinned up on her head in an elaborate arrangement of curls. Her face was faintly heart-shaped, dominated by as compelling a pair of dark green eyes as Longarm had seen in a long time. That face had a faintly puzzled smile on it as she came toward Longarm with her hand extended.

"M'sieu?" she murmured in a throaty voice. "You wish to speak to me?"

There was no sign of recognition on her face. Was it possible she hadn't heard Gullen talking about him to her brother? Maybe she didn't know they had a federal lawman after them.

Maybe she didn't even know anything her brother was up to. Rostand could have kept the whole thing from her in order to protect her. She might believe that the two of them were simply on some sort of excursion trip, although she must have wondered why they would check out of the Menger and leave San Antonio at night like they had.

All he could do now was try to brazen it out, he thought. He smiled and took Jeanne's hand, saying, "Yes, mademoiselle. I'm very glad to meet you."

Behind him, the clerk piped up, "I thought you said the Rostands were your friends."

Longarm ignored him, kept hold of Jeanne's hand, which was as cool and smooth as he would have expected, and steered her toward the open rear doors of the lobby. "You were about to go for a walk, weren't you?" he said with a nod toward the parasol in her other hand. "Maybe I could join you."

"But of course." She still looked and sounded puzzled, but she was much too genteel and ladylike to cause a ruckus. As they emerged onto the rear galley, facing the water, she went on in a slightly chiding tone, "You're not one of those men who wants only to do business with my brother, are you?"

"No, not at all. I want to take a walk beside the water on a beautiful evening with an even more beautiful woman at my side."

She laughed. "I warn you, M'sieu . . . ?"

"Long," he told her.

"I warn you, M'sieu Long, I have been flattered by some of the most charming men in all of Europe. As intriguing as you are, do you think a Texas cowboy can match words with them?"

So his pose as a gentleman hadn't fooled her. Well, he wasn't surprised. His suit was fairly cheap, and the deep, permanent tan on his face testified to a life spent mostly outdoors.

"You don't quite have it right, ma'am," he said. "I'm not from Texas, and I'm not a cowboy."

"Then where are you from?" she asked. Her voice carried a faint accent, but her English was excellent.

"A place called West Virginia," he told her. "West-by-God Virginia, we always called it, but I don't reckon you'd care about that."

"Of course I care. I find all you Americans fascinating, especially those of you here in the West. You are so much different from the men I have always known. So much more earthy. So much more dangerous."

She linked her arm with his as they strolled across the lawn, and he felt the soft, warm pressure of her breast against his sleeve.

Dadgum if the little French gal wasn't flirting with him!

Longarm got his mind back on business, which really wasn't difficult considering how much pain and death and suffering the gal's brother had been responsible for. An idea had begun to form in the back of his head. He didn't like it much, but fate had presented him with an opportunity and he might be a fool not to take advantage of it.

"What brings you to our country?" he asked as they walked past a flower bed toward several thick-trunked and wind-twisted live oak trees bunched where they overlooked the water.

"Business, of course. The only reason my brother ever goes anywhere or does anything." She looked up at him. "Are you *sure* you are not one of Maurice's associates?"

"I've never met him," Longarm replied honestly.

"It's just that there are two other men . . . he had some sort of dealings with them in San Antonio, and they have come with us here to Rockport. And they remind me of you."

Longarm didn't like hearing that he reminded anybody of a pair of torturing, murdering skunks like Gullen and Shifflet, but he didn't let that reaction show. Instead he forced a chuckle and asked, "Are they earthy and dangerous, too?"

"Not earthy, not so much. But definitely dangerous. I do not like them, M'sieu Long, but Maurice says they must go with us on the *Bellefleur*, and the old Mexican gentlemen as well."

"The *Bellefleur*?" he repeated.

"*Oui*. Maurice's yacht."

So that guess had been right. They would be sailing away from Rockport in a private vessel.

That was their plan, anyway. Longarm was going to have something to say about that.

They had reached the trees and moved into the thickening shadows underneath them. Longarm glanced back toward the hotel about a hundred and fifty yards away. As the sky purpled with evening, the lights around the big building grew brighter. He doubted if anybody on the galleries or looking out a window inside the building could see him and Jeanne under the trees, and there was nobody near them on the lawn.

He was about to suggest that they stop when she saved him the trouble by saying, "I think we have gone far enough, M'sieu Long."

"That's fine, mademoiselle."

"My brother would be very angry with me if he knew I had gone walking with a perfect stranger, and an American, at that. He may be looking for me even now."

"I don't want to cause any trouble for you, ma'am."

Now that was a lie, sort of. He didn't necessarily *want* to cause trouble for Jeanne if she didn't know what was going on, but he was sure going to.

"You asked for us by name, and yet you admit you do not know either myself or my brother," she said. She sounded like she was starting to get suspicious now.

"I heard about you and your brother staying at the Austin House, and I thought it would be nice to meet you and maybe take you for a walk by the water."

She stood facing him, close to him so she had to tip her head back to look up at him. She was a little bit of a thing . . . but a mighty nice little bit.

"You wanted to meet a French woman," she said, sounding a little accusatory. "You have heard all the stories and wanted to know if they are true."

"Stories?" Longarm said. She couldn't mean—

"You wanted to know if I would suck your cock," Jeanne said.

The blunt, crude words coming from the sweet mouth of this lady hit Longarm like a punch for a second. He sensed that she was trying to shock him, and he wasn't going to give her the satisfaction of showing her that she had.

"Ma'am, you mistake my intentions," he began.

"No, M'sieu Long, you mistake mine. You see, this is the first time I have been able to slip away from Maurice ever since we have been in this godforsaken country, and I want very much to see if the things I have heard about you American men are true."

This wasn't going at all the way Longarm had expected it to. It veered off the tracks even more when Jeanne stepped closer to him, dropped her parasol, and reached up to wind both arms around his neck. She had to lift herself on her toes to reach his mouth with hers as she kissed him.

Her mouth was so hot and sweet and urgent that he couldn't help but react. He felt himself stiffening, and the way her belly was pressed against his groin, she had to be feeling it, too. She broke the kiss and reached down boldly to explore him through his trousers.

An exclamation in soft French came from her. "It *is* true!" she said. "American men have cocks like horses!"

"Now hold on a second," Longarm said.

Her fingers flew to his trouser buttons. "I must see it for myself."

He clenched his teeth and moved his hands to her wrists, grasping them firmly and stopping her from unfastening those buttons.

"You got to stop that," he said.

She looked up at him in surprise. "You do not want me to—"

As a matter of fact, he wanted very badly to let her take

as much of his shaft into her sweet little mouth as she could, but something was wrong here. Maybe she really was just a gal with a wanton nature out for a good time . . .

Or maybe this was a damn trap.

A sudden rush of footsteps told him that his instincts had been right to warn him. He shoved Jeanne away from him and whirled toward the men who rushed toward him from the shadows. One of them ordered harshly, "Get him!"

Longarm didn't want to start a shooting match with Jeanne so close by, even if she *was* a treacherous little minx who had decoyed him out here so those varmints could jump him. The men attacking him didn't seem to want gunplay, either. The closest one swung a fist at him.

Longarm ducked under the punch and closed in to hook a hard right fist into the fella's belly. The man gasped and doubled over. Longarm grabbed his shoulders and slung him into a couple of the others charging toward him. All three of them went down in a sprawling tangle.

Unfortunately, that still left two more men on their feet, and one of them landed a blow on Longarm's jaw that sent the big lawman staggering backward. He caught his balance as the other man rushed in, then lifted a foot into the man's groin. Outnumbered five to one, there was no way he was going to worry about fighting fair.

The man let out a high-pitched whine and clutched at himself. As he started to fall, he gasped, *"Merde!"*

That was French for "Oh, shit!" Longarm thought. Maybe these varmints were crewmen from Rostand's boat.

He straight-armed a punch into the face of another man. The ones he had knocked down were scrambling up, apparently unhurt. They started to close in around them.

He had lost sight of Jeanne. She had probably run off after doing her treacherous job. That meant he didn't have to worry about hitting her if he loosed any shots, so he palmed out the Colt and was about to order the men to back off before he started blasting.

Before he could do that, one of the sons of bitches kicked the gun right out of his hand. Jessie Starbuck's half-

Japanese friend and bodyguard, Ki, could do things like
that, and evidently so could these Frenchmen. Longarm's
right hand had gone numb from the impact of the kick
against his wrist, but his left still worked fine. He crashed it
into the jaw of one of the other men and sent him spinning
off his feet.

The odds against him were simply too much. Every time
he knocked one of the men down, another leaped in to take
his place. Longarm couldn't block all the punches. A fist
caught him on the ear. Another thudded hard into his chest
and knocked him back.

He ran into the massive, gnarled trunk of one of the live
oaks. That was actually a lucky break. He pressed his back
against it. Now his attackers could only come at him from
the front. He had flexed the fingers of his right hand enough
to get it working again, so he threw a punch with it and
knocked one of the men back a couple of steps. He followed that with a left hook to the jaw of another man.

But their assault was relentless. A punch drove Longarm's head back against the tree trunk behind him. The
double impact made red rockets go off behind his eyes.
Stars pinwheeled through his brain, even though he couldn't
see the actual stars from here under the trees. A fist drove
into his midsection and made him hunch his shoulders as
sickness exploded in his belly.

Something hammered down on the back of his neck,
driving him to his knees. Strong hands grabbed his arms,
jerked him up again. More punches slammed into his stom-
ach and ribs as two of the men held him. Consciousness
was slipping away from him now, and he barely felt the
blows, savage though they were.

Then they stopped abruptly, as a man's silky smooth
voice commanded, "Enough."

Rostand. Longarm wasn't sure how he knew the voice
belonged to the Frenchman, since he had never heard it
before, but there was no doubt in his mind.

The voice spoke again, and from the tone of it Longarm
could tell the man was issuing more orders. The words were

in French. He couldn't follow them. Rostand might be ordering the men to kill him, for all Longarm knew.

Then darkness closed in around him, and he didn't know anything anymore.

Chapter 13

Awareness bloomed in Longarm's brain like the slow opening of a flower. There was nothing pretty about it, though, and it sure as hell didn't smell sweet.

In fact, the smells that filled Longarm's nostrils were those of seawater and dead, rotting fish. That stench, and the way whatever he was lying on rocked slightly underneath him, told him that he was on board a boat.

It took him a minute or two to figure out this must be Maurice Rostand's yacht and to remember that the vessel was called the *Bellefleur.*

Pretty flower . . . not hardly.

Pain rolled like thunder through Longarm's head. He kept his eyes closed, figuring the darkness was a blessing right now. Nor did he try to move. Somebody might be watching him, and if they were, he didn't want them knowing just yet that he had regained consciousness. A groan wanted to well up his throat, but he forced it back down.

Instead he listened intently, hoping to get some clue what was going on around him. He heard the faint slap of water against something, probably a boat's hull, which confirmed his hunch about his location. But that was all. No voices, no sounds of anybody moving around.

Maybe he was alone.

He risked opening his eyes, prying the lids up with an effort like that of trying to lift a couple of boulders. It didn't do any good. Even though he knew his eyes were open, he couldn't see anything except utter blackness.

So he was somewhere in a windowless room, on a boat. A cabin on the *Bellefleur*, or maybe the cargo hold? That seemed likely to Longarm. He was Maurice Rostand's prisoner.

Well, at least you ain't dead, old son, he told himself. He wasn't sure why they had kept him alive after Gullen had tried so hard to kill him in San Antonio, but right now he was thankful for small favors like continuing to draw breath.

The pain in his head and the aches in his body had subsided a little. He was thinking more clearly now. His arms were pulled back behind him uncomfortably, and when he tried to move them, he couldn't. His hands were tied.

His feet seemed to be free, though. He could move his legs.

Since he seemed to be alone in here, he pulled his knees up and then pushed with his feet, sliding himself along the floor. After he had done that a couple of times, the top of his head bumped against something when he tried it again. He rolled onto his side and wriggled his way up into a sitting position with his back pressed against a wall of some sort. Then, after a moment spent catching his breath, he began testing the bonds around his wrists in an effort to see if there was any chance he could work himself loose.

Long minutes dragged by, and finally Longarm was forced to admit that he wasn't going to be able to wriggle out of the ropes. He had been tied up by somebody who knew what he was doing. One of the sailors on the *Bellefleur*, more than likely.

That meant he had to start looking for something he could use to help free himself. He pressed his back harder against the wall, got a foot under him, and struggled to stand. When he was upright, a wave of dizziness hit him. He had to lean against the wall and wait for it to pass.

"Son of a bitch," Longarm muttered. It didn't make him feel any better.

When he felt steady enough to move again, he slid along the wall, keeping a shoulder against it so he wouldn't get disoriented in the darkness. The wooden surface was his only anchor to reality in this stygian gloom.

He hadn't gone very far when his shins barked painfully against something. He explored it as best he could with a booted foot and decided it was a crate of some sort. He turned around and dropped to his knees so he could explore behind him with his bound hands.

If he could find a way to get hold of the crate's lid well enough to pry it off, it might have a nail in it he could use to pick away at the ropes around his wrists until he loosened them. It would take hours, but he didn't know how long he had been down here or how long it would be before anyone came to check on him. He might have enough time.

His fingers were a little numb because the ropes around his wrists were tight. He fumbled at the crate, searching for a spot where he could slip his fingers into a gap and wrench the lid loose. Frustration grew inside him as he didn't find what he was looking for.

Suddenly, Longarm's head lifted as he heard footsteps above him. Somebody was walking across the deck. Were they coming down here?

He didn't know, but if they were, he didn't want them to realize that he was trying to escape. He could always find his way back to the crate later. He surged to his feet and moved along the wall away from it as the footsteps stopped.

Seconds later, with a faint creaking sound, a hatch lifted. Light spilled down into the hold, blinding Longarm. His eyes had grown accustomed to the blackness.

He blinked as he stood against the wall, or bulkhead, or whatever the hell it was. As his sight began to adjust to the glare, he made out a ladder being lowered into the hold through the hatch in the ceiling.

A man climbed part of the way down the ladder, then

reached up and took a lantern from someone else. He descended the rest of the way and turned to face Longarm, holding the lantern up so its light filled the space.

It was indeed a cargo hold, as Longarm had guessed. Quite a few crates and barrels were scattered around, although there was a lot of open space, too. Longarm saw that through narrowed eyes and then turned his attention toward the man with the lantern.

The man was tall and brawny, dressed in white canvas trousers and a tight blue shirt. Probably the uniform of a crewman on the yacht, Longarm realized. The man's jaw thrust out belligerently, and his nose had been broken at least once, sometime in the past. He glared at Longarm for a second before looking up and calling something in French through the open hatch.

The man pulled a pistol from behind his broad black belt and pointed it at Longarm as he came forward.

"I don't reckon you need that gun," Longarm told him. "I ain't in much shape to put up a fight."

The man stepped to one side and said something else in French. Another pair of legs began climbing down the ladder, this time in sharply creased, expensive-looking dark trousers.

The pants went with the rest of the suit, the white shirt, the silk cravat with a jeweled stickpin holding it in place. The man wearing the fancy duds was slender and of medium height, Longarm saw as the man reached the bottom of the ladder. He had sleek dark hair and was handsome in a predatory way, Longarm saw as the man turned toward him. Longarm put his age around the mid-thirties.

"Marshal Long," the newcomer said. He continued in excellent English, "We finally meet."

"M'sieu Rostand," Longarm said.

The man inclined his head in acknowledgment. "I regret that our introduction has to come in such unpleasant circumstances. You are such a dogged individual I cannot help but feel some admiration for you. You are an American version of the indomitable Inspector Javert, no?"

"Never heard of the hombre," Longarm said. "Is he some French star packer?"

Rostand waved a hand. "Never mind. I'm impressed that you were able to follow us here to Rockport. I hoped that we would successfully mislead you into going to Corpus Christi."

"I'm pretty good at followin' the smell of skunk."

Rostand's eyes narrowed slightly in anger, but he said, "You should be grateful to me, rather than insulting, Marshal. M'sieu Gullen wanted to kill you out of hand, but I decided that I wanted to interrogate you. I'd like to find out how much you actually know, and how much information you have passed on to your superiors."

As a matter of fact, Longarm hadn't wired Billy Vail with anything he had found out so far, but Rostand didn't have to know that.

"What you're sayin' is that you want to ask me some questions and *then* kill me."

Rostand gave an eloquent shrug of his narrow shoulders. "You have been quite an annoyance so far, Marshal, you cannot deny that. If not for you, I might not have an . . . unwanted partner, shall we say."

"You mean Gullen wouldn't tell you who I am until you agreed to let him horn in on your game, is that it?"

Rostand ignored the question and came a step closer. "Tell me, Marshal . . . do you know the secret of the Star of Father Cristobal?"

Longarm stared stonily at him and didn't say anything.

After a moment, Rostand looked over at the sailor and said, "Andre."

The big man handed Rostand the lantern and the gun, then clenched his fists and moved toward Longarm. Longarm knew what was coming, so he didn't just stand there and wait for it.

Instead he lowered his head and lunged forward, ramming the top of his skull into the sailor's chest with unexpected speed and force.

Taken by surprise, Andre flew backward. Longarm had

tried to butt him into Rostand, which might have caused the Frenchman to drop the lantern and start a fire, which Longarm could then have used to burn through the ropes on his wrists. It was a mighty slim chance but better than nothing.

Rostand jumped nimbly aside, though, and Andre sprawled on the deck next to some of the cargo. He didn't look happy at all as he climbed back to his feet.

Longarm dodged the first blow, but the second one caught him on the jaw and sent him reeling back against the wall. Andre moved in and slammed a fist into his belly. Longarm fell to his knees. Andre took hold of his shirt and dragged him up on his feet again. He held Longarm against the wall with one hand and cocked the other fist behind his head.

"I assure you, Marshal, it can get much worse," Rostand said. "Do the wise thing and tell me what I wish to know."

Longarm didn't say anything.

Rostand sighed. "All right, Andre. Go ahead."

One thing about getting the hell beat out of you . . . after a while you went a little numb and the punches didn't hurt as much. When Andre finally stopped throwing them and let go of Longarm's shirt, the big lawman slid down the wall until he was sitting again. His mouth was full of blood.

Rostand set the lantern on a crate and came over to lean down in front of him. "What do you know about the Star of Father Cristobal?" he asked.

"God ain't gonna like it," Longarm mumbled through swelling lips, "you stealin' one o' His sacred relics like that."

Rostand let out a contemptuous snort. "God has nothing to do with it, Marshal."

"M-miracle . . . miracle the old padre . . . survived."

"Not at all," Rostand said with a shake of his head. "Lucky, yes, but not miraculous. And now the good fortune of Father Cristobal's discovery will be mine."

Longarm had no idea what that meant, but his brain was still working well enough despite the beating and he was able to file away Rostand's mention of the old priest's "discovery." That might be important later . . . if he lived.

"Were you in touch with your superiors?" Rostand prodded. "What did you tell them?"

Instead of answering the questions, Longarm muttered, "That was pretty sorry of you . . . old son . . . sendin' your little sis after me . . . as bait like that. Did you tell her to . . . say them nasty things to me?"

Rostand's eyes widened and his face flushed with anger. "Do not talk about my sister," he snapped. "Jeanne has nothing to do with this!"

"She's the one who lured me . . . out to them trees . . ."

"I had a man watching for you in case you showed up, even though I didn't expect you to. He said that you had gone walking with Jeanne, so I sent my men to find you as quickly as possible. If you laid one hand on her, I can promise that your death will be a painful one, Marshal."

So all that talk about giving him French lessons really *had* been her own idea, Longarm thought. He was a mite surprised. But he had long since learned not to be too shocked at anything a gal came up with. They were the most unpredictable breed on the face of the earth.

It was a shame he probably wouldn't get to help her find out what she wanted to know about American men.

Lips drawn back in a snarl, Rostand took hold of Longarm's shirt and twisted it. "Well?" he demanded. "Did you touch my sister?"

"Take it easy," Longarm said. "We just walked and talked, and then your fellas jumped me. I didn't do anything to her, and I didn't tell her about the Star."

Rostand let go of him. Longarm slumped back against the wall. "You have just bought yourself a small bit of mercy," the Frenchman said. "*If* you are telling the truth. But I still want answers to my other questions."

Longarm looked past him, saw yet another pair of legs coming down the ladder. Joshua Gullen skipped the last couple of rungs and dropped to the deck. Rostand looked around at him and straightened.

"What does it matter who Long told?" Gullen demanded. "As soon as we sail, we'll be out of his jurisdiction. Won't be any other federal badge toters able to come after us, either."

"I want to know," Rostand said stubbornly. "Your government could file a protest with the Mexican government—"

Gullen sliced the air with his hand. The cut on his face made him uglier than ever.

"The Mex government isn't gonna give a damn about any protest from Washington. They've got plenty on their plate as it is."

"No word of what we're after can come to their ears," Rostand insisted. "If they knew, they would interfere."

Gullen thought about it for a second and shrugged. "You're probably right about that. You may not be able to make this muleheaded lawman talk, though. Why take a chance? Kill him right now and be done with it."

Rostand took out a silver pocket watch that looked like it had probably cost a small fortune. He opened it, checked the time, and said, "We sail at dawn. That is less than four hours away. If Long has not talked by the time we reach international waters, his body goes overboard. That way no one will ever find it, and there will be no questions about a dead lawman."

"Fine," Gullen said. "When the time comes, I wouldn't mind being the one to kill him."

"We shall see." Rostand stepped away and made a small gesture to the big sailor. "Andre."

Andre grabbed Longarm and jerked him to his feet. Longarm stretched his bruised, bloody face into a grin and said, "Too bad little Jeannie won't get to suck my cock like she wanted to. I'll bet she gets mighty tired of suckin' all your little bitty French dicks, includin' her brother's."

Rostand swung around with a furious French oath. He didn't have to give an order. Andre drew back his fist and smashed it into Longarm's face. Longarm went back against the wall and slid down it to lie in a limp, crumpled heap.

Rostand stood there breathing hard for a long moment before he got control of his rage. "Idiot," he muttered, but it wasn't clear whether he was directing the imprecation toward Andre or himself. "He is unconscious again. Now we will have to wait to ask him more questions."

"I'm tellin' you, you ought to just go ahead and cut his throat," Gullen said. "I'd be glad to do it for you."

"No." Rostand jerked a hand toward the ladder. "Andre, get the lantern. We will leave him here and come back later, when he has regained consciousness. There will still be plenty of time before dawn."

"But one way or another . . ."

"At dawn he dies," Rostand agreed.

Chapter 14

From where he lay on the floor against the wall, Longarm listened to the men climb out of the hold and pull the ladder up after them. He wasn't unconscious at all, although his jaw ached like a son of a bitch where Andre had walloped him.

He had been moving his head away slightly when the punch hit him, so it hadn't landed with quite as much force as the big sailor had thought it did. The impact was still powerful enough to make Longarm see shooting stars for a second, but he hadn't blacked out. It had looked like it, though, from the way he made all his muscles go limp and collapsed.

That was exactly what he wanted his three captors to think.

He slitted his eyes just enough to see darkness close in again as the hatch cover was lowered. He listened intently but didn't hear anybody dog it into place. Why would they bother? As far as they knew, he was out cold and didn't have any way to reach the hatch anyway with the ladder gone.

While Andre was beating him and Rostand was questioning him, Longarm had been looking around. He had spotted one of the supply crates that looked like it had been

opened for some reason, then had the lid hammered back
down on it but not as carefully as before. He had marked
the location in his mind as best he could. Now it was a matter of seeing if he could find it in the dark.

He didn't have any time to waste. They probably wouldn't
leave him alone down here for more than an hour, if that
long, before they came back to see if he had regained consciousness. He gave them a minute or so to get away from
the immediate vicinity of the hatch, then struggled up onto
his feet.

Carefully, trying to make as little noise as possible, he
shuffled across the hold in what he hoped was the right
direction. He ignored the pain that wracked him. If he
didn't find the crate he wanted on the first try, he didn't
know if he would ever be able to find it. The thick darkness
was utterly disorienting.

His left leg bumped against something. He stopped,
moved that leg back and forth as he tried to trace the di-
mensions of the object. It was a crate, he decided. Now he
had to find out if it was the right one.

He turned and lowered himself, reaching out blindly with
his hands. His fingertips brushed rough wood. He leaned
back and explored the top of the crate. Was there a gap anywhere along the lid?

Yes! Longarm's breath hissed between his teeth. The
opening was a tiny one, not even big enough for him to get
his fingers completely in it, but he was able to get a grip on
the lid and lift up on it.

The side of the crate he had hold of came up off the
floor. This wasn't going to work, he thought bitterly. He
had to brace the crate somehow so he could try to prise up
just the lid.

He slid it backward, again trying to be quiet about it.
The crate moved a foot or so, then came up against something solid. Longarm was hunkered with his back to it, so
he came up on his toes and moved back enough so the heels
of his boots rested against the side of the crate. The position
was awkward as hell and he didn't know if it would brace

the crate well enough for his purposes, but he had to give it a try. He set himself, got the fingers of both hands in the little gap around the lid as much as he could, and heaved.

The lid moved, and the rest of the crate didn't. Not much, but enough to send hope surging through him.

He got ready and heaved again. This time he heard a faint squealing sound as nails shifted in the wood. He could get his fingers all the way into the gap between lid and crate now.

Longarm paused, drew in a couple of deep breaths. When he was set, he pressed his heels against the side of the crate and lifted on the lid with all the strength he could summon from his battered frame. The nails squealed again and suddenly let go. The lid flew up and off the crate and landed somewhere nearby with a clatter. The abrupt lack of resistance threw Longarm off balance and made him sprawl awkwardly on the deck.

He lay there with the blood pounding inside his skull. Somebody up on the yacht's deck could have heard that clatter and might come down to investigate. Not only that, but the lid had fallen somewhere and he couldn't see it.

Longarm waited to see if anyone was going to respond to the racket. His blood froze in his veins as he heard footsteps crossing the deck. Several tense seconds dragged past, and the footsteps faded without coming anywhere near the hatch.

He had dodged one more bullet.

When he had heard the crate lid fall, he'd had enough presence of mind to try to determine its location. He sat up and scooted in that direction. After a minute or so, something jabbed his hip. He twisted around and fumbled at it with his bound hands.

It was the lid, and just as he had hoped, one of the nails was sticking up where he could get at its sharp point.

He couldn't afford to work at the ropes for hours on end. Instead he used the nail to gouge at them, hoping to hook strands and pull the knots loose. Sometimes he missed and jabbed the point into one of his wrists instead, and he could feel his skin growing slick with the blood that oozed from the wounds. As long as he didn't do something stupid like puncture a vein, a little blood was a good thing. Might make it easier to slip out of the bonds.

Longarm had no real way of judging the passage of time. He just gouged and pulled at the ropes as much as he could, stopping every now and then to twist his wrists and see if he had gotten any play in the ropes. He didn't put too much pressure on them. He didn't want to tighten the knots even more.

Finally he felt the ropes slip a little. He kept doing what he was doing, and the next time he twisted his wrists, the bonds slipped even more. Impatience suddenly welled up inside him. He bunched the muscles in his arms and shoulders and pulled on the ropes as hard as he could.

They parted, and those muscles shrieked in protest as he brought his hands around in front of him. He flexed his fingers, willing them to work properly.

Longarm dragged deep breaths into his body. He reached over and felt around for the wall, then leaned on it to brace himself as he heaved up to his feet. He ought to still have a few lucifers in his vest pocket. He fished one out and managed to snap it alight, although it took him a couple of tries.

He couldn't afford to leave the match burning. Somebody might notice the glow coming through the tiny gaps around the hatch cover. So in the second or two that he could see, he narrowed his half-blinded eyes and looked around, locating himself and the things he needed. He shook the match out and dropped it on the floor.

Then he set to work, forcing his battered body to do what he told it.

Working by feel, he started stacking crates. It wasn't easy in the dark to build a tower that wouldn't fall down and cause such a racket they would hear it all the way to Corpus Christi. After every crate that he put in place, he had to test the structure for steadiness before he moved on to the next step.

When he thought what he had built was tall enough, he

climbed on it carefully. He didn't know what was going on abovedecks, but he knew it was sometime in the wee hours of the morning and he hadn't heard anybody moving around for a while. Except for one or two men on watch, maybe everybody on the *Bellefleur* was asleep.

Longarm's plan was to slip out through the hatch onto the deck, go overboard without anybody seeing him, and swim to shore. Once he was there, he would get the local law, the Texas Rangers, hell, anybody he could find who was willing to help him, and storm the yacht, taking Rostand and his confederates prisoner.

Or killing them, as the case might be. Longarm didn't really care about that anymore.

He was reaching up for the hatch cover to see if he could ease it back a little when he heard hard footsteps approaching. Biting back a curse, he waited and hoped whoever it was would go on, as they had before.

No such luck. With a grating sound, the hatch cover opened above his head.

As it turned out, his aim had been a little off in the darkness. That was the only thing that saved him. He was standing a little behind and to one side of the opening. The ladder came down, and a man started climbing down it.

Longarm recognized the white trousers and blue shirt of the yacht's crew. A second later, Andre's rugged face came into view. A look of shock appeared on it as he spotted Longarm standing there on the stacked-up crates.

Longarm was already thrusting his arm *through* the ladder and reaching for the sailor. Before Andre could make a sound, Longarm's hand closed around his throat and jerked him forward. Andre's nose slammed into one of the rungs and popped again, spurting blood. Longarm kept his hand clamped like an iron vise around the man's throat so Andre couldn't yell.

The sailor had the pistol tucked behind his belt. That was a fatal mistake. Longarm's other hand plucked the gun free. He reached around the ladder and brought it crashing against Andre's skull. He felt bone give under the blow.

Andre sagged and his feet slipped off the ladder. Longarm couldn't hold his weight up one-handed. He had to let go.

Andre fell the rest of the way to the floor of the cargo hold. Luckily, it was only a few feet. He made a considerable thump when he landed, but maybe not loud enough to be heard outside unless someone was close by and listening for it, and Longarm had heard only one set of footsteps approaching the hatch. Rostand had probably sent Andre by himself to see if the prisoner had regained consciousness yet.

The crates started to sway under Longarm's feet. The struggle with the sailor had unbalanced the crates a little. Longarm threw his arms out to the side and crouched, trying to find the right balance point to make the crates stop swaying. After a nerve-wracking few seconds, they did so.

Longarm swung himself around to the other side of the ladder and climbed down.

It took him only a moment to check for a pulse and make sure Andre was dead. He started pulling the sailor's clothes off. Blood from Andre's broken nose had splashed over the front of his shirt, but it might not be noticeable from a distance.

Less than a minute later, Longarm climbed the ladder again, this time wearing the dead man's clothing. Andre had dark hair but no mustache, so Longarm kept his head down as he emerged from the hatch. He pulled the ladder up and moved the cover back into place, just as Andre would have done if he had gone below and found the prisoner still out cold. If anyone was watching, he didn't want them getting suspicious.

A couple of lights burned fore and aft on the yacht. A large cabin bulked in front of him. Rostand and Gullen were in there somewhere, he thought, along with Jeanne.

It occurred to him that Gonzago was probably locked up in one of the cabins, too. Clearly, the old man was important to Rostand for some reason, probably because Gonzago still hadn't translated the writing on the Star, so Rostand wouldn't toss him in a cargo hold the same way he would a prisoner he intended to kill soon.

What would happen to Gonzago when the forces of the law boarded the yacht to arrest everyone? Chances were, Rostand and his men would put up a fight. Gullen almost certainly would. With bullets flying around, the old man would be in danger. It was even possible that Rostand might kill him just to be sure that no one else would ever discover the secret of the Star. It would be an evil thing to do . . . but Maurice Rostand was an evil son of a bitch.

Longarm knew he had to try to find Gonzago and get him off the boat before all hell broke loose. If anything happened to the old man, he might never know what this was all about.

In the dim light, he saw the door into the cabin. He headed that way with a resolute stride, as Andre would have done if he were going to report to his employer. Longarm opened the door and found that it led into a dimly lit corridor with several doors on each side. At the other end of the corridor were double doors. He supposed that some sort of salon or dining room or main cabin lay behind them, with the bridge beyond that.

The quarters back here had to be the staterooms where guests slept. Guests . . . and important prisoners.

How the hell was he going to figure out which one Gonzago was locked up in?

As he asked himself that, the question itself suggested a possible answer. The door to Gonzago's room would be locked. The others might be, too, but Rostand probably felt pretty safe on his own boat. Jeanne likely did, too.

So if he found a locked door, either a harmless old Mexican or a cold-blooded killer would probably be on the other side of it. That was one hell of a choice.

Longarm had to make it, though.

He had found a small clasp knife in the pocket of Andre's uniform trousers. He figured he could use it to slip the lock on whichever door he chose to try first. He reached out to the closest knob on his right and carefully wrapped his fingers around it to see if it turned.

It didn't. Longarm took the knife from his pocket and

opened it. He slid the blade into the tiny gap between the lock and the strike plate and started probing. The operation didn't make much noise, only a few tiny scratching sounds.

But they were enough to attract the attention of the room's occupant, who must have been awake already. Longarm pulled back as soft footsteps rapidly approached the door. A key rattled in the lock.

That ruled out Gonzago. If the old man was locked in, he sure as hell wouldn't have a key.

Longarm started to turn away. Maybe whoever was in there would see the uniform and take him for a member of the crew. Not likely, but . . .

The stateroom door swung open, and Jeanne Rostand said, "Andre? Andre, is that you?"

Longarm and the dead sailor were about the same size, wearing the same clothes, and both had dark hair. Maybe he could pull off the ruse, Longarm thought as he grunted noncommittally and acted like he was going to move on down the corridor.

But Jeanne laughed softly, grabbed his arm with both hands, and tugged him toward the door, saying, "Andre, this is foolish. What if my brother finds out? Still, this may be our last chance to make love before the boat sails . . ."

Well, son of a gun. Andre had been bedding the boss's hot-blooded little sister. The room was dark and Longarm still might have tried to get away from her without revealing who he really was, but she wrapped her arms around his neck and pressed her mouth hotly to his.

Only to jerk back, gasp, and cry out, "You are not—"

She didn't finish the sentence. Her mouth opened wide to let out a scream. Longarm lunged after her and tried to clamp his hand over her lips to silence her, but her lithe body twisted away from him.

A blood-curdling shriek rang out, filling the stateroom and probably echoing from one end of the *Bellefleur* to the other.

Chapter 15

A bitter curse ripped from Longarm's mouth. He leaped toward Jeanne again. The lamp in the stateroom was turned low, but there was enough light for him to see that she wore a gown of thin, emerald green silk that clung enticingly to her sweet little body.

Longarm didn't have time to appreciate the view. Jeanne had reached a dressing table and snatched a single-shot derringer from the top of it. Longarm caught her wrist and forced it up just as she pulled the trigger. The tiny gun went off with a pop and sent its bullet into the ceiling.

Longarm wrapped his other arm around Jeanne and swung her off her feet like she didn't weigh anything. He plunged toward the door. His shoulder hit the teakwood panel and slammed it outward with considerable force.

The door smacked into a sailor who was rushing toward it. The stunning impact sent the man reeling across the corridor, where he ran into Joshua Gullen, who was just emerging from that stateroom. Their legs tangled, and Gullen went down howling a curse. The hired killer shoved the sailor aside and lifted the gun in his hand as Longarm made a dash for the main deck with a still-screaming Jeanne Rostand slung over his shoulder.

His plan to rescue old Gonzago was shot to hell now, but

at least he had an unexpected bargaining chip. A pretty redhead, at that. He heard Gullen's gun cock behind him, but before the man could pull the trigger, Maurice Rostand shouted, "No! Hold your fire! You might hit Jeanne!"

That was what Longarm had hoped would happen. He ran out on deck. One arm was wrapped firmly around the squirming young woman. He headed for the closest railing and stopped when he got there, swinging around to face the yacht's main cabin. Dawn was still an hour or more away, but the eastern sky had begun to turn gray with the approach of a new day.

Rostand, Gullen, and a big man who had to be Shifflet came boiling out of the door, followed by several members of Rostand's crew. Guns bristled in the hands of Gullen and Shifflet.

Rostand signaled sharply for everyone to stop. "Don't shoot," he said.

"Maurice!" Jeanne cried as she stopped struggling for the moment. "Maurice, help me! This madman has me!"

"I see that," Rostand said. "Long, do not hurt my sister. If you do, I swear I will kill you."

"I ain't interested in hurtin' your sister," Longarm said.

That statement prompted Jeanne to renewed fury. She twisted around and swatted at Longarm's head. "You . . . you crack-brained brute!" she shouted. "Maurice told me you have been following us for days because you wanted to kidnap me! I cannot believe I thought even for a moment that you were a nice American cowboy!"

Longarm slid Jeanne off his shoulder in front of him and caught her wrists. He pulled her against him, turning her so that her back was snugged up to his body.

"Settle down, gal!" he snapped at her. "Your brother's been lyin' to you."

That brought a torrent of French from her, probably curses that a lady like her shouldn't even have known.

"Let her go, Long," Rostand said. "She has nothing to do with what is between us."

"You want her back, I'll trade you." It went against the

grain for Longarm to hide behind anybody, especially a woman, but he had a job to do and he had to play the cards the way they were dealt to him. "I want the old man. Bring him out, put him in a little boat, and have a couple of your men row him to shore."

Longarm had seen that the *Bellefleur* was anchored about a hundred yards offshore, rather than being tied up at one of Rockport's docks. The yacht was considerably larger than most of the fishing craft that called this their home port.

"Once Gonzago is safe," he went on, "the boat can take me and your sister ashore. I'll let her go there and the boat can bring her back out here to you."

Coldly, Rostand said, "You are insane. You are outnumbered twenty to one. You cannot dictate terms, and you cannot hope to escape, Marshal."

That little slip on Rostand's part brought a gasp from Jeanne. "Marshal!" she repeated. "You mean this man is a gendarme, not a lunatic?"

"I reckon there's a whole heap of things your brother ain't told you, ma'am," Longarm said.

Rostand took a step forward. Even in the dim light, his face was an icy, implacable mask. "You cannot have the old man," he told Longarm. "I still need him. But you can save your own life. Release Jeanne, and you can have safe passage ashore."

Longarm didn't believe that for a second. He knew that as soon as he didn't have Jeanne's body shielding his anymore, Gullen and Shifflet and the sailors who were armed would fill him full of lead.

"No deal," he said. "I get Gonzago, or you don't get your sister back."

"What are you going to do?" Rostand smiled. "Kill her?"

"Wouldn't take me but a second to snap her neck," Longarm warned.

"And then what? We kill you, of course. You know that. You know you are not leaving this ship alive, Marshal, but there is no need for my sister to die."

Longarm felt Jeanne's small breasts heaving against his

arm as she breathed harder. "Maurice, what are you saying?" she asked. "What is this about? Why is that . . . that old Mexican so important?"

"I'm sorry, Jeanne. You don't know what's at stake here. It is more than you can possibly imagine."

Longarm said, "Looks like you ain't as important to your big brother as you thought you were, mademoiselle."

"You . . . you pig!" she spat. Her heart pounded hard in her chest. Longarm could feel it with no trouble at all through the thin silk of the nightgown.

"I am truly sorry," Rostand said. He turned his head slightly to order the crewmen, "Prepare to sail."

"But M'sieu Rostand," one of them said, "it is not yet dawn—"

"Do as I say!" Rostand barked. "We leave now!" He turned back to Longarm and Jeanne. "But before we go, we must make sure we are not followed."

Gullen and Shifflet lifted their heavy revolvers.

"No!" Jeanne cried. "Maurice, no! You cannot—"

Longarm didn't wait for her to finish her protest. He knew the two gunmen were about to open fire. He tightened his arms around Jeanne and threw himself backward. He toppled over the railing, taking Jeanne with him, as Gullen and Shifflet blasted shots toward them.

The slugs whipped through the space Longarm and Jeanne had occupied a heartbeat earlier. They plummeted toward the water. Another lusty scream issued from Jeanne's mouth. Longarm kept one arm tight around her body and clamped the other hand over her mouth and nose so half of Aransas Bay wouldn't wind up inside her when they hit the water.

They landed with a huge splash and went deep under the murky surface. Jeanne panicked and started trying to fight her way free of his grip. He wouldn't let her go. Grateful for the fact that his clothes and boots were helping to hold them down under the surface, Longarm started kicking hard and hoped that he was propelling them in the right direction.

He heard some odd little *vip! vip!* noises through the water that pressed against his eardrums and realized that what he was hearing were bullets cutting through the water, searching for them. Gullen and Shifflet were firing blind, though. The bay was too dark for anybody to see them.

Something else made a larger splash. Longarm figured Rostand had ordered a small boat put over. He would be sending men out to look for them, but he couldn't afford a lengthy search. He had already given the order to raise the anchor and get the ship ready to sail, and Longarm was sure he would go through with it.

Rostand had been prepared to have his own sister killed rather than give up his chance at whatever it was he was after. It was a cinch that he would be willing to abandon her and make a run for it if he had to.

Longarm's lungs were starting to feel the strain of being underwater, and he had thought to grab a deep breath as he was falling from the yacht. Jeanne had been too busy screaming to do that. She was still trying to get loose, but her struggles were growing feeble.

Longarm decided he couldn't wait any longer. He kicked for the surface.

Their heads came out of the water. He took his hand away from Jeanne's mouth and she gasped desperately for air, dragging it into her lungs. Longarm waited a second, then clamped his hand over her lips again. He left her nose uncovered this time, though, so she could still breathe, even though she couldn't yell.

They hadn't made much noise when they surfaced. Longarm looked around and listened, trying to locate the small boat that was searching for them. After a moment he spotted it about fifty yards off to their left. One of the sailors in the boat had a bull's-eye lantern and was shining it around.

Longarm put his mouth next to Jeanne's ear and whispered urgently, "Listen to me! I want to help you. Your brother was willing to kill you to get what he wants. You saw that with your own eyes!"

She shook her head as if denying what he told her. Angry noises came from behind the hand over her mouth.

"It's true and you know it," Longarm persisted. "The old man is more important to him now than you are."

This time she didn't shake her head. Maybe he was getting through to her.

"If you'll let me help you, I'll get you ashore safely," he promised. "You got to stop fightin' me, though. I think that fella's gettin' ready to shine that light over this way, and we got to go under again. Are you ready?"

A second's hesitation, and then she nodded.

Longarm hoped she was telling the truth.

The man with the bull's-eye lantern started to swing it toward them. "Take a deep breath," Longarm told Jeanne. He took his hand away from her mouth. Now he would see whether or not she believed him.

She didn't scream. She hauled in a deep breath, just like he was doing, and then they went down together, sinking beneath the dark surface.

Longarm tilted his head back and saw the light from the lantern skitter along the gently lapping waves above them. He hoped Jeanne had enough sense to hold her breath. Air bubbles popping on the surface could still give them away.

The light probed the water around them for a maddeningly long time, but finally it went away. Longarm heard the little splashes as oars dug into the water. Maybe the searchers in the small boat were giving up and returning to the yacht.

He stroked with his free arm, sending them drifting to the surface. They floated with just their faces above the water, breathing air that smelled wonderful to them despite the lingering odors of rotting fish.

The eastern sky was considerably lighter now. Longarm could see that he and Jeanne were about halfway between the *Bellefleur* and the shore. The sailors who had manned the small boat were climbing up a rope ladder to the yacht's deck. Longarm faintly heard their voices as they reported to

Rostand, but they were speaking French and he couldn't make out the words.

Jeanne must have heard some of them well enough to understand them, though. "Drowned," she said. "They told Maurice they think we must have drowned."

"We came a mite closer than I'd like," Longarm said as the water lapped around his face and tried to get into his mouth and nose. He spit some of it out.

Someone on board the yacht shouted an order.

"I . . . I do not believe it," Jeanne said. Longarm could hear the misery in her voice, along with the disbelief. "Maurice is telling the crew to set sail. He is abandoning me!"

"Listen to me, Mademoiselle Rostand. I'm a deputy United States marshal. Custis Long is my name. It's true that I followed you and your brother down here from San Antonio, but that's because he's mixed up with some criminals."

"M'sieus Gullen and Shifflet," she said bitterly. "I never liked them, never trusted them."

"And you were right not to," Longarm told her. "They're both killers. They kidnapped that old man who's been traveling with you, and they murdered a young woman in San Antonio to get some information out of her."

"Maurice could not have known—"

"He paid them to do it," Longarm broke in, being deliberately blunt, even brutal, about it in an effort to get through to her. "They're working for your brother."

"No, no . . ." Jeanne murmured. But despite the denial, he could tell she was starting to understand that what he was saying had to be true. She began to shiver.

"This water's gettin' mighty cold," Longarm said. "Let's get to shore."

On the *Bellefleur*, sails snapped and billowed as the wind caught them. The ship began to swing around and move away from shore, its silhouette visible against the lightening sky.

Jeanne watched it go, and Longarm thought he saw a

couple of tears roll down her cheeks. Her face was so wet already that he couldn't be sure, though.

"M'sieu Long . . . Marshal Long . . . you will help me? I am not so good a swimmer."

"I'll help you," Longarm said, and tightening his arm around her again, he began to stroke for shore.

Chapter 16

Jeanne was still shivering a little as she sat in the local marshal's office with a blanket wrapped around her and sipped from a cup of hot coffee. Longarm stood nearby with his own cup, wishing he had a little Maryland rye with which to sweeten the brew. That would have done an even better job of warming him up.

The local star packer, a middle-aged man with a drooping white mustache, frowned at Longarm. His name was Foster, and he wasn't convinced by Longarm's story.

"How do I know you're really federal law, like you say?" he wanted to know. "You ain't got no badge or identification papers."

Longarm sighed. "I told you, they're on that boat that sailed off a while ago. I left 'em in my coat when I changed clothes with the fella who was wearin' this sailor suit."

Longarm was still clad in the white trousers but at least most of the blood had come off the blue shirt during his swim. He had clean clothes in his war bag at the boarding-house where he'd rented a room, but Marshal Foster wasn't inclined to let them go just yet.

The marshal had been waiting on the dock when Longarm and Jeanne climbed out of the bay. The gunshots fired by the men on the *Bellefleur* as the two of them made their getaway had echoed all across the waterfront of the peaceful town and drawn plenty of attention. Foster had been rousted out of bed by complaints of a small war breaking out and wasn't happy about it. Nor had he been satisfied with Longarm's answers so far.

In a way, Longarm couldn't blame him. Even though he knew that Rostand and Gullen were responsible for stealing the Star of Father Cristobal, kidnapping old Gonzago, and murdering Mercedes, he still had no idea what was behind all of it. It had to be something mighty important to have caused so much mayhem, though.

Foster tugged on one side of his mustache and said, "Maybe I ought to just lock the two of you up until I get all this sorted out."

"Let me send a wire to Chief Marshal Vail in Denver and it'll get sorted out a lot quicker," Longarm said.

Foster thought it over and slowly nodded. "I reckon I could do that."

"And you really need to let the lady go back to the hotel so she can get some dry clothes on. They can tell you there that she's really Jeanne Rostand."

"They can tell me that she's *registered* as Jeanne Rostand, maybe," Foster said. "There's a difference."

"Dadgum it." Longarm was losing his temper with this overly cautious local. Rostand and the *Bellefleur* were getting away, and he had to do something about it.

But what? He didn't know where they were going.

Jeanne might, though. It was important that he have a talk with her, in private, as soon as possible.

"You're right about the lady, though," Foster went on. "'Tain't civilized to make her sit around in wet clothes." He sniffed in disapproval. "Skimpy clothes, at that. Tell you what I'll do. You say you're stayin' at the Austin House, ma'am?"

"*Oui*, m'sieu," Jeanne said.

"Well, you sure *sound* French, I'll give you that. I'll send one of my deputies down there with the two of you so you can get cleaned up, but he's gonna stay on guard in the lobby, so don't even think about tryin' to get away."

Longarm was about to point out that he wasn't staying at the Austin House, but before he could say anything, Jeanne caught his eye and nodded, then said, "Thank you so much, M'sieu Foster."

"While you're gone, *I'll* send that wire to Marshal Vail in Denver. That way I'll know that everything's on the up-and-up."

The deputy Foster assigned to them was a big young man named Charlie Hoyt. He didn't seem too bright, but he was friendly enough, despite the loaded shotgun he carried tucked under his arm.

With the blankets Foster had loaned them still wrapped around their shoulders, Longarm and Jeanne walked toward the hotel, drawing a lot of curious stares from the folks who were up and about already on this new day. Charlie trailed behind them with the Greener.

"We still have a suite in the hotel," Jeanne said quietly to Longarm. "You can come up with me and I'll send a porter to fetch your clothes. I . . . I really do not wish to be alone right now, Marshal Long."

"Reckon I can understand that," Longarm said. "You've been through a lot."

"Yes, I think being betrayed and abandoned by one's own brother counts as 'a lot.'"

Longarm couldn't argue with that. He hoped that under the circumstances, Jeanne would be willing to help him, not to mention able. Any lead she could give him would be better than what he had now, which amounted to nothing more than a hunch that Rostand was headed for somewhere in Mexico. Whatever was behind all this had to be tied in with the old padre's arduous trek a hundred and fifty years earlier.

A different clerk was on duty at the desk in the Austin House lobby than had been there the previous evening, but he recognized Jeanne. "Mademoiselle Rostand!" he exclaimed when he saw her wet, bedraggled appearance. "What in God's name happened to you?"

Jeanne didn't explain. She just lifted her chin and said with as much dignity as she could muster, "I do not wish to discuss it, m'sieu. Please, could I have the key to our suite?"

"Why, sure." The man took the key from the rack and slid it across the desk. He frowned at Longarm. "I don't believe—"

"He is with me," Jeanne said before the clerk could go on.

In the face of that imperious declaration, the man could only nod and say, "Oh. Of course." Then he looked at the deputy. "Charlie Hoyt, what are you doing here?"

"I'm with them, too," Charlie said.

Jeanne turned to him. "But you will wait for us here in the lobby," she said. "I heard Marshal Foster say so."

Charlie thumbed his hat back on his head. "Yeah, I reckon that's right." He added sternly, "I'll be waitin' right down here."

Longarm and Jeanne went up the stairs. Under his breath, Longarm said, "Nice young fella, but he ain't any great shakes as a guard."

"Do not blame him." She smiled up at him, the first smile he had seen from her since the night before. "Most men do whatever I ask them to do."

"Yeah, I ain't surprised," Longarm said, remembering that she had been carrying on with Andre and who knew how many other members of Rostand's crew. He hadn't mentioned to her that he had killed Andre in the course of his escape, and he wasn't planning to bring it up.

"You think you are immune to my charms?"

"I didn't say that." Longarm figured she was falling back into her old flirtatious ways because it helped her to not think about what had happened.

They reached the suite on the second floor. Jeanne gave Longarm the key and let him unlock the door. He didn't think anybody would be lurking inside to jump them, but it didn't hurt to be careful.

The fancy sitting room was empty, and so were the two bedrooms, he saw when he quickly checked them out. He nodded to Jeanne and said, "All right, you can get cleaned up and in some dry clothes now."

"*Merci*, Marshal." She tossed the blanket into a corner of the sitting room, and as she started through the door into her bedroom, she pulled the silk gown up and over her head, giving Longarm a good look at the smooth sweep of her back and her pertly rounded ass before the door swung closed behind her.

A moment later, the door opened again and she stuck her head back out, revealing a bare shoulder. "You can go in Maurice's dressing room. There are towels there, and a robe."

Longarm didn't think any robe worn by Maurice Rostand would fit him, but he could dry off, anyway, and maybe wrap a towel around himself. He nodded to Jeanne and said, "Much obliged."

He went into the small dressing room off of Rostand's bedroom and found a stack of thick, fluffy white towels. Stripping off the soggy sailor's uniform, he kicked the duds into a corner and started toweling off vigorously. When he was dry, he checked the robe that was hanging on a hook, but as he suspected, it was much too small for him.

The towels were big enough that he was able to wrap one of them completely around his lean waist and tuck it in. When he had done that, he wandered back out into the sitting room. He found Jeanne there.

Rather than getting dressed in dry clothes, she had done like he had and wrapped one of the towels around herself, although hers was wrapped and tucked so that it covered her breasts. Her hair was still damp and hung in auburn curls around her shoulders.

"We must talk, Marshal," she said. "I have already rung for a porter and sent him for your things, so we have some time."

Longarm nodded. "Obliged for that, too. And I was thinkin' the same thing. I reckon you want to hear the whole story, or as much of it as I know, anyway."

"I do," she said, her voice firm.

Longarm noticed a faint tremble in her chin, though.

"This ain't a pretty yarn," he warned her. "You're gonna hear some things you probably won't want to hear. Things you won't want to believe."

"I am not the foolish, innocent child my brother has always believed me to be. Just tell me the truth, Marshal."

Longarm did. As he spoke, Jeanne paled at times and finally sat down on a padded hassock in front of the divan. The towel was short enough that it left her slim legs bare from the knees down, and he thought she looked mighty attractive sitting there like that. He had more important things on his mind than some gal's legs, though.

When he had finished, she looked up at him and asked, "What do you intend to do now, Marshal?"

"Well . . . if I can figure out where your brother and those gun wolves who are with him took the old man, I reckon I'll go after 'em."

"But there is a matter of jurisdiction, is there not? You are a United States marshal."

"Is that your way of tellin' me that your brother is headed for Mexico?"

"You did not answer my question."

Longarm shrugged. "Yeah, I guess when you get down to it, my jurisdiction ends at the Mexican border . . . unless Billy Vail works something out with the Mexican government givin' me the authority to operate down there, which ain't likely to happen since it hardly ever has in the past. But just between you, me, and the bedpost, I've been known to bend the rules a mite, every now and then."

"So you *are* going after them, whether it is legal or not."

"They stole that relic, kidnapped an old man, and killed a girl on American soil," he said, and he couldn't stop a slight note of harshness from entering his voice. "I don't know about legal, but I figure that me trackin' 'em down and seein' that they get what's comin' to them is damn sure justified."

For a long moment, she didn't say anything. Then, softly, "I agree with you."

"So you'll help me?"

"*Oui*." Her voice was barely above a whisper. "What do you want to know?"

"Did your brother ever say anything about where he was going from here?"

"He never told me such things . . . but I heard him talking to M'sieu Gullen. I heard him mention a place called San Ramon. I have no idea where it is."

"San Ramon . . ." Longarm repeated. The name was vaguely familiar to him. He was willing to bet that he could find somebody who knew where it was.

"But how can you go after him?" Jeanne asked. "You would need a boat, and someone to sail it."

Longarm smiled. "I don't reckon either of those things are in short supply around here." He paused. "What *is* in short supply is the cash to hire what I need. My boss is willin' to look the other way sometimes when I don't do things strictly by the book, but there's no way in hell he's gonna send me a wad of Uncle Sam's money to go chasin' off to Mexico. And as for me personal-like, I've got enough dinero in my war bag to buy a handful of cheroots, maybe, but that's about all."

"So you are poor."

Longarm chuckled. "You could say that."

"I just did. Fortune has smiled on you again, Marshal. I am rich. I have cash of my own put away in my baggage that Maurice does not know about."

"And you'd be willing to let me use it to charter a boat?"

"On one condition."

Longarm frowned. "And what might that be?"

"That you take me with you."

That was the answer he was expecting, all right. He started shaking his head and said, "That just ain't a good idea—"

Jeanne got to her feet and did something to the towel wrapped around her. It fell to the floor around her feet, leaving her standing there nude in front of him.

She smiled at him and said, "The idea, she is beginning to sound better, no?"

Chapter 17

Longarm was as human as the next hombre. He couldn't help but look at the pert, tip-tilted breasts with their small pink nipple, the smooth curves of Jeanne's hips and thighs, and the inviting triangle of auburn hair at the juncture of her thighs. He couldn't but appreciate what he saw, too.

But that didn't mean he was going to go along with being blackmailed into agreeing with her.

"No, it still ain't a good idea," he told her, keeping his voice flat so she wouldn't know how much the sight of her was affecting him.

Her eyes flashed angrily. "Did you not hear me?" she demanded. "I will not let you have the money to hire the boat unless I come along, too."

"It's too dangerous," he insisted. "We don't know for sure where your brother is going, or why he's headed there."

"I could stay in San Ramon," she suggested.

Longarm shook his head. "It's probably just a scruffy little Mexican seacoast town. No place for a lady like you."

"My brother was going to take me there with him, remember?"

"That don't mean I'm goin' to."

She glared at him and stomped her foot, which made it a

little easier for him to ignore the fact that she was naked as a jaybird. A little easier . . . but not much.

"You are a . . . a stubborn American!"

"You called me a crack-brained brute earlier," Longarm said with a smile. "I sort of like that."

"I did not know you as well then."

"That was only a couple of hours ago," he pointed out.

"And a great deal has happened since then, has it not?" Her voice caught as she went on, "My world has been, how do you say, turned upside down since then."

Longarm frowned. She was right about that. She had discovered that not only was her brother a dangerous criminal, but also that he cared more about whatever it was he was after than he did about her. Right now she had to feel almost totally alone in the world, deserted, without a friend.

Except for him.

No wonder she didn't want him to go off and leave her here in Rockport. He could put her on a boat that would eventually take her back to France, if she had enough money to pay for that passage as well as chartering the vessel that would take him to Mexico, but she would be alone there, too.

Still frowning, he tugged at his earlobe and scraped a thumbnail along his jawline. After a moment, he said, "I reckon we could at least find out something about San Ramon before we make up our minds. It might not be too bad a place for you to wait for me."

A brilliant smile flashed across Jeanne's face. "Yes!" she said as she practically jumped at him. She clasped her arms around his neck and wrapped her legs around his hips as she kissed him. He felt the hard nipples on those little breasts of hers prodding his bare chest. Instinctively, his arms went around her ripe bottom to support her.

He still had the towel wrapped around him, but his cock was standing up like an iron bar by now and threatened to dislodge it. She ground her pelvis against the shaft through the towel and made it slip even more. When she rubbed one of her heels against it behind him, the towel lost its precarious hold entirely and dropped to the floor around his feet.

That meant his cock now jutted between her thighs with nothing to keep the top of it from rubbing against the slick opening between her legs.

She clung to him and pumped her hips back and forth, sliding the lips of her pussy along the shaft. Her mouth opened to Longarm's probing tongue, and a passionate moan welled up from deep inside her. Longarm wouldn't have thought it was possible, but he got even harder.

She pulled her mouth away from his and gasped, "Like this, Marshal Long! Standing up, no?"

"Yes," Longarm said as he grasped her hips and moved her, adjusting her position. "And considerin' what we're about to do, I really think you ought to call me Custis."

"Oh, yes, Custis. Put that big American cock in me now!"

Longarm wasn't going to argue with a request like that, or deny it, either. He lifted Jeanne a little so he could get the best angle, then lowered her onto his shaft. The thick pole of flesh spread her wide as he entered her. He thrust harder as the hot, buttery walls of her sex enclosed him.

At this angle, he couldn't get all of his cock inside her, but it was still enough to make her cry out, "*Mon dieu!* Never have I been filled like this!"

She leaned back, grasping his shoulders to steady herself. His hands under her ass held her up with no trouble. She worked her hips so that his shaft slid wetly in and out of her. Her heels dug into the small of his back.

Longarm felt her begin to spasm after only a few moments. He understood, because his own climax was about to thunder through him. He didn't try to hold it back. Instead he pulled Jeanne harder against him and drove his cock into her as far as he could as it began to explode.

In a series of deep, throbbing bursts, he emptied himself inside her. At this angle, the thick fluid mixed with her juices and welled right back out, drenching both of them. Longarm shuddered as he finished off. So did Jeanne.

They were both left breathless and sweaty. In this humid

climate along the coast, any sort of exertion would get you overheated in a hurry, and they had just exerted a whole heap. With her arms and legs still wrapped around him, Jeanne rested her head on Longarm's shoulder and tried to catch her breath.

When she could speak again, she said, "Now we have to . . . clean up again."

"Yeah," Longarm agreed.

She lifted her head. "I have an idea. I will wash you, and you will wash me."

"If we try doin' that, we're liable to get even sweatier," Longarm pointed out.

She pouted prettily. "You are right, of course. And we have other things to do. Important things." His shaft had slipped out of her. She took one arm from around his neck and reached down to grasp it. "But when we get a chance, I want to see how much of this I can get in my mouth. I have the reputation of the French people to uphold, you know!"

"I'll hold you to that," Longarm said.

The porter brought Longarm's war bag to the Rostand suite a short time later. Longarm dressed in jeans and a faded blue work shirt. "I'll have to buy another hat and Colt and gun rig," he said as he rolled the shirtsleeves up a couple of turns on his brawny forearms.

"Then you are lucky I have plenty of money," Jeanne said with a mischievous smile. She was dressed in a summery frock. Her auburn hair was pulled back behind each ear and held in place with tortoiseshell clips. She looked as beautiful and innocent as a spring day.

"I can put gear like that on my expense account," Longarm said. "My boss won't complain about it too much."

"I thought you had only enough to buy, what was it, a handful of cheroots."

Longarm shrugged. "I've got a little emergency dinero stashed in my war bag. Just not enough to charter a boat."

She offered him her arm. "Well, then, shall we go and tend to our business?"

The morning was getting away from them, and the *Bellefleur* was putting more and more distance behind it with each passing minute.

"Let's go," Longarm said.

On their way downstairs, Jeanne asked, "What about M'sieu Charlie Hoyt, the deputy?"

"I reckon we'll have to give him the slip. If Marshal Foster knew we were fixin' to light a shuck, he'd toss us in the hoosegow for sure."

Jeanne frowned up at him. "Was that English you just spoke, Custis?"

"Well, sort of," he said with a chuckle.

They didn't have to worry about getting away from the deputy. Charlie Hoyt was waiting for them at the bottom of the stairs with his shotgun tucked under his arm. With a worried frown, he said, "Y'all were up there a mighty long time. What were y'all doin'?"

"Hatchin' a plot to get away from you, Charlie," Longarm told him.

The young man waved a hand. "Oh, you can forget about that. Marshal Foster come by a few minutes ago. He'd got a wire back from your boss in Denver that said you was who you claimed to be, right down to that fancy mustache o' yours. The marshal still wants to talk to you, but he said for you to come back by his office at your convenience."

Longarm nodded and said, "Thanks, Charlie." He didn't intend to waste any more time palavering with the local lawman, though. Instead he asked the deputy, "Do you know anybody around here who's got a boat big enough for a sea voyage who'd be willin' to hire out?"

A smile wreathed Charlie's friendly face. "Why, sure. You need to go talk to my uncle Valentine. Happens he's in port right now. Does passenger and freight business between here and New Orleans and Cuba. I reckon you could charter his boat if the price was right, though. You tell him Charlie sent you."

"What's the boat's name?" Longarm asked.

"He calls it the *Ozar.*" Charlie shrugged. "Don't ask me why. I ain't got a clue."

He told them how to find his uncle's boat, and then Longarm said, "You can tell the marshal we'll be by later today to talk to him. In the meantime, there's no need to say anything about what you told us about your uncle."

Charlie nodded. "Sure. I reckon that's private business 'twixt you and Uncle Valentine."

Charlie shook hands with him and said so long. As the two of them left the hotel, Jeanne said, "We should be ashamed of ourselves, taking advantage of that young man's good nature and gullibility."

"Yeah, Charlie's liable to get yelled at when Foster finds out we've sailed away, but he'll get over it. Your brother's already got too big a lead for us to sit around jawin' with some nosy star packer."

Jeanne laughed. "I have a feeling that being around you is going to be an education, Custis, in more ways than one!"

"I can teach you how to find trouble, all right," Longarm agreed. "I'm damn good at that."

It didn't take them long to locate the *Ozar*, an elderly two-masted schooner that looked like someone had taken good care of it. Longarm stood on the dock beside a gangplank and called, "Hello, the boat! Permission to come aboard?"

A stocky man with a short, grizzled beard emerged from the schooner's forward cabin. He lifted a hand in greeting and said, "Howdy, folks. What can I do for you?" As an afterthought, he added, "Oh, yeah, come on aboard."

Longarm and Jeanne went up the gangplank with Longarm holding her arm to make sure she didn't topple off into the water that washed the dock's pilings. When they reached the deck, he said, "We're lookin' for the captain of this boat."

"That'd be me. Cap'n Valentine Wood." He held out a hand.

Longarm shook with him. "Your nephew Charlie Hoyt sent us."

"Ah, Charlie. My sister's boy. A good heart, but not quite a full complement of sails, if you know what I mean. You folks aren't in trouble with the law, are you? Charlie's a deputy."

"Not hardly," Longarm said. "In fact, I *am* the law. Deputy U.S. Marshal Custis Long."

Wood didn't ask for identification, and Longarm was glad of that. The captain's bushy white eyebrows rose in surprise, though, and he asked, "What can I do for Uncle Sam?"

"You know a place called San Ramon?"

Without hesitation, Wood nodded. "I do. Little town about a hundred miles down the Mexican coast. I've put in there from time to time."

"We need somebody to take us there."

Wood turned curious eyes on Jeanne. "And who might this lovely lady be?"

"Mademoiselle Jeanne Rostand," Longarm introduced her.

Cap'n Wood took Jeanne's hand, and danged if he didn't lean over and kiss the back of it. "Enchanted, mademoiselle," he murmured.

"You have charming manners, Captain," she said.

"I've spent considerable time in New Orleans." Wood frowned. "I heard talk about some yacht anchored here that belonged to a fella named Rostand."

"My brother," Jeanne said. "He sailed early this morning."

Wood looked surprised again. "And didn't take you with him?"

"It's a long story," Longarm said. "Can you take us to San Ramon?"

"Is that where the lady's brother is headed after runnin' out on her?" The captain held up a hand. "No, never mind, that ain't any of my business. It just so happens I *can* offer you passage to San Ramon, but it'll cost you."

"We are prepared to pay," Jeanne said.

"You got a crew ready to go?" Longarm asked.

Wood waved a hand to take in their surroundings. "I know this ol' tub so well I don't need much of a crew. But I got three Cubans. They're ashore right now, and it'll take me about an hour to round them up and get ready to sail. You folks in any bigger hurry than that?"

"That'll work," Longarm said.

Wood's pale blue eyes narrowed. "I got a feelin' maybe this voyage ain't entirely on the up-and-up, even with you bein' a lawman and all."

"You don't have a thing to worry about," Longarm told him. "You just take us to San Ramon, and your job is done."

Wood thought about it for a moment, then shrugged and nodded. "Hope you got your sea legs," he said. "We set sail in an hour."

Chapter 18

The voyage to San Ramon was uneventful, except for the two nights at sea Longarm and Jeanne spent in Jeanne's cabin exploring every inch of each other's bodies and doing just about everything a man and woman can do together. And when it came to what the French ladies were famous for, Jeanne did her sisterhood proud.

She had no trouble with seasickness, either. Having traveled the world with her brother, she was accustomed to being on his yacht. Longarm, on the other hand, had never been much of a seagoing man, but his iron constitution kept him from getting sick.

The wind was fair, the sea calm, and the *Ozar* handled well. Captain Valentine Wood and the three Cuban crewmen had no trouble with the schooner. During one of the days when they were at sea, while Longarm was standing at the boat's railing smoking a cheroot, the captain struck up a conversation with him and explained that the schooner was named after the hero of an ancient Aztec legend.

"A fierce and bloody people, them Aztecs," Wood mused. "If they hadn't died out for whatever reason it was, they might have wound up rulin' the world by now. We might have human sacrifices in every town in the country. Some fella who owns a hardware store might put on a fancy feathered headdress every month or so, take out a bone knife, and carve the still-beatin' heart out of a livin' virgin."

Longarm looked askance at the burly captain, who shrugged.

"Roamin' the seven seas, as I done for nigh on to forty years, you hear a lot of strange stories."

"I reckon so," Longarm muttered.

The settlement of San Ramon perched along the curving shore of an inlet, on land carved out of a thick forest of tropical trees. The vegetation didn't extend very far inland, though, as Longarm could see as the *Ozar* approached the port on the third day after leaving Rockport. The terrain began to rise almost immediately into a series of rolling hills, which turned into a band of sere, rocky ridges before ascending abruptly to a range of medium-sized but extremely rugged-looking mountains.

San Ramon didn't look like the sort of town where a wealthy adventurer like Maurice Rostand would find anything he was looking for. It was a squalid settlement of perhaps a thousand people who subsisted largely on fishing, although Captain Wood explained to Longarm that there were some farms in the inland hills and that there was also some trade in timber from the forest.

"The harbor's pretty shallow," Wood explained as the three of them stood at the railing while the Cubans handled the sails. "We'll drop anchor a ways offshore and signal for 'em to send out a boat to take you in."

Longarm's eyes were searching among the ships tied up in the harbor. One of them was anchored a short distance out, like Wood intended to do with the *Ozar*, and Longarm's jaw tightened a little as he recognized the *Bellefleur.* He had never gotten a good look at the vessel in daylight, but he figured it was the only rich man's yacht that would be docked in San Ramon.

He pointed it out to Jeanne, who looked both sad and angry. "Maurice is here," she said dully.

"Maybe, maybe not," Longarm said. "He could have traveled on inland. He would have left the yacht here so he'd have a way to leave whenever he gets what he's after." He turned to the captain again. "Is there a hotel in this town?"

"Aye. It's run by a fella called Leopardo. 'Tain't a fancy place, and it ain't what you'd call spic and span, neither, but it's not too bad for a burg like San Ramon. When ol' Leopardo hears that you come in on the *Ozar*, he'll treat you right."

Chances were, if Rostand was still in town, he would be staying at the hotel, Longarm thought. That meant he and Jeanne would have to be careful. He didn't want Rostand and Gullen knowing they were in San Ramon just yet.

"Cap'n, you're laying over here tonight, aren't you?" he asked Wood.

"Yeah, I thought I would. We can take on more fresh water and supplies, and maybe I can pick up some cargo to carry back to New Orleans, even though with what you're payin' me, I could sail back empty and still turn a profit on the trip." Wood chuckled in satisfaction at the deal he had negotiated.

"Then don't signal for that boat to take us ashore just yet. If it's all right with you, I reckon Mademoiselle Rostand and I will stay on board until after dark."

Wood regarded him shrewdly. "Afraid there might be somebody waitin' for you, eh?"

"Keepin' an eye out for us, anyway, just in case we show up."

Wood made an expansive gesture. "It don't matter none to me when you go ashore. That's up to you."

"Obliged," Longarm said. "We'll be out of your hair soon."

Wood took off his cap and ran his hand over his mostly bald scalp. "Ain't much hair to be out of!" he chortled.

They dropped anchor, and several small boats came out even though Wood hadn't signaled for any. The people of San Ramon were always glad to see a ship sail into their harbor.

Longarm and Jeanne stayed out of sight in their cabins until nightfall. He wouldn't put it past Rostand to be using field glasses to scan the decks of any vessels that arrived. He knew the men who had searched for him and Jeanne in Aransas Bay had told Rostand they were probably drowned, but Rostand might not want to take any chances.

Longarm wondered if the son of a bitch had shed any tears over the possible death of his sister. He wouldn't have wanted to bet a hat on it.

Once darkness had settled down over the harbor and the town, Wood came to Longarm's cabin and knocked on the door. "I talked one of the fellas into leavin' his boat here so we could use it," the captain reported. "I can have a couple o' my boys row you and the lady ashore now."

"Just me," Longarm said. "The lady's stayin' on board."

Hearing Longarm and Wood talking, Jeanne opened the door of her cabin in time to hear the big lawman's statement. She exclaimed, "*Non!* You are not going to bring me all the way down here and then send me away, Custis!"

"Settle down," Longarm told her. "I should've said, you're stayin' on board for now. I'm gonna go ashore first, get the lay of the land, and see if your brother is still in town."

"Oh," she said. "I suppose that will be all right. Just do not even think of, how would you say it, double-crossing me."

"Never occurred to me," Longarm lied. The truth was that he had thought about locking her in her cabin and sending her to New Orleans with Captain Wood. Whether he did or not depended to a certain extent on what he found in San Ramon.

Longarm went down a rope ladder to the small boat manned by a couple of Wood's Cuban crewmen. They unshipped the oars and sent the little craft sculling over the dark water toward San Ramon.

Quite a few lights burned in the town. When Longarm climbed out of the boat onto one of the docks, one of the Cubans asked him, "Do we wait here for you, señor?"

"Yeah, give me an hour or so," Longarm said.

"And if you are not back by then?"

"I can't very well ask you to come lookin' for me. That ain't your job."

He saw white teeth in the moonlight as both sailors grinned. "No, señor, but we never run away from a fight or a beautiful woman. We will come to the hotel and see what we can find out."

"*Gracias*," Longarm told them.

Captain Wood had told him how to find the hotel. In a settlement the size of San Ramon, it wouldn't have been that difficult even if he hadn't had directions. The hotel was a two-story building of whitewashed adobe and stucco with a red tile roof. It was the largest structure in town except for the timber warehouse on the edge of the settlement, and definitely the most impressive-looking.

Longarm stayed in the shadows as much as possible as he approached it. At this time of night, there weren't many people on the streets, and he knew a gringo of his height would draw some attention unless he stayed out of sight as much as possible. He worked his way to the mouth of an alley across the street from the hotel and lingered there, watching the few people who were coming and going.

He didn't see anybody he recognized. No Rostand, no Gullen, no Shifflet. After about fifteen minutes, though, he spotted a man in the white trousers and blue shirt that marked the uniform of the *Bellefleur*'s crew.

That made sense. The captain of the yacht probably kept most of the crew on board in order to maintain discipline, but at the same time, he might be facing a mutiny if he didn't allow the men to come ashore, probably three or four at a time, to enjoy whatever vices San Ramon had to offer.

The sailor ought to be able to tell him whether Rostand and his gun wolves were still on board the yacht, here in town, or somewhere else entirely, Longarm decided. Still sticking to the shadows, he began following the man.

The sailor acted like he knew where he was going. This was probably at least his second trip ashore. Longarm trailed him to a small, squalid cantina with a row of cribs out back.

The question was whether the sailor was after liquor or a woman. Longarm had a hunch it was a woman. He circled the building to keep an eye on the cribs.

He didn't have to wait very long before the sailor emerged from the rear door of the cantina with his arm around a shamefully young Mexican girl in a dirty cotton shift. They went to one of the cribs and disappeared inside.

Longarm would have liked to kick the door down and interrupt the fella's fun, but that would cause more of a commotion than he could afford. Instead he waited, knowing there was a good chance that when the sailor finished and left, the girl would linger behind to clean herself and make sure he had left enough money.

After about ten minutes, the door of the hovel opened. There wasn't much light back here, of course, but enough filtered through the open back door of the cantina for Longarm to recognize the sailor suit. Whistling happily through his teeth, the Frenchman started back toward the building.

Longarm stepped out, looped his left arm around the hombre's neck, and jabbed the barrel of his new Colt into the man's back.

"Don't make a sound, old son," Longarm grated in the man's ear, "or I'll blow your backbone in two. You'll never stick that pecker of yours in some poor little girl again."

The lawman's arm was clamped so tightly across the sailor's throat that he couldn't talk. He started to struggle, though, and Longarm pressed harder with the gun muzzle.

"I know you probably got a knife hid away somewhere. I promise you, you can't get it out and stick me before I can kill you." Longarm dragged him deeper in the shadows. "Now come on, if you know what's good for you."

He had no idea if this French sailor understood English, but a gun in the back and a threatening tone were damn near universal. The man stopped fighting. Longarm hauled him all the way to the far end of an alley where no one was around.

Then he took the gun away from the sailor's back, but only to reverse his grip on it and rap the butt sharply against the man's skull. The sailor fell to his knees, stunned. Longarm kicked him in the back and drove him forward on his face.

It took only a moment to pull the man's belt off and use it to lash his wrists together behind his back. He couldn't get up from the position he was in now. As awareness came back to him and he realized his face was pressed to the filthy dirt floor of an alley, he began to sputter in French. Longarm hunkered on his heels and silenced the racket by pressing the cold ring of his gun barrel against the man's temple.

"That's better," Longarm said. "You speak English?"

"*Oui*," the sailor gasped. "A . . . a little."

"You know who I am?"

"The . . . the American lawman?" the sailor guessed. "The one who killed Andre?"

"That's right, and I'll kill you, too, old son, if you don't tell me what I want to know. I'll shove this gun in your ear so it won't make much noise and blow your brains right out the other side."

"*Non!* No, please, m'sieu! Please do not kill me!"

The alley smelled so bad already it was hard to distinguish any new smells, but Longarm was pretty sure he got a whiff of fresh urine. The sailor was so scared he had pissed himself. That was good.

He leaned closer. "Where are Rostand, Gullen, and Shifflet?"

Miserably, the sailor said, "M'sieu, I . . . I cannot betray my employer. M'sieu Rostand, he is a hard man. If he knew I helped you, he . . . he would kill me!"

"If you don't tell me where I can find him, you'll already be dead, *monsieur*."

Longarm drew out the French word menacingly. The sailor started to sob. Longarm jabbed the gun muzzle against the man's ear.

The sailor started to writhe around in panic. "No, no! I will tell you! Do not shoot!"

"Talk fast, old son."

"M'sieu Rostand and the two American gunmen, they are not here. They hired men and horses and pack animals and went inland. I do not know where, I swear it!"

The answer didn't surprise Longarm, but he wanted to be sure the man wasn't trying to trick him. "How do I know you're tellin' me the truth?"

"Ask the man who runs the hotel! M'sieu Rostand paid him to help organize the journey! On God's holy name, m'sieu, that is the truth!"

"A fella who beds gals that young, even whores, hadn't ought to be swearin' on God's name," Longarm growled. He pulled the gun away from the man's ear and stood up.

"I have t-told you what you wanted to know," the sailor panted. "You cannot leave me here like this. There are vermin, and the people of this town, they are thieves, if any of them find me helpless like this they will kill me!"

"Yeah, I reckon that's true." Longarm holstered his gun and reached down to grasp the man's arms and haul him to his feet. He didn't want to leave the man here to be murdered, but neither did he want to free him so the sailor could go back to the *Bellefleur* and alert the rest of the crew that Longarm was not only alive but also in San Ramon. Rostand might have left orders for them to stop him. "You're comin' with me."

"M'sieu . . ."

"That or a bullet in the head."

"*Oui.* I . . . I will come with you."

Longarm marched the sailor back to the dock where he had left the Cubans with the small boat. One of them said, "We were about to come looking for you, señor. Who is this?"

"He's comin' with us back to the *Ozar.* Cap'n Wood can put him to work, or keelhaul him, or whatever he wants to do."

Longarm had thought it over on his way back to the waterfront. When the sailor didn't return from his visit ashore, the captain and the rest of the crew of the *Bellefleur* would probably think that he had either been robbed and killed in some alley or had gone native. Either way, they might look for him, but the mere fact of his disappearance wouldn't alert them to Longarm's presence in San Ramon.

The oars splashed quietly in the water as the Cubans rowed back out to the schooner. The prisoner sat in front of Longarm, shivering in fear.

When they reached the *Ozar*, Longarm climbed on board first and pulled his gun to cover the French sailor as the man clambered up the rope ladder to the desk. Jeanne and Captain Wood were waiting. Jeanne gasped in surprise as she recognized the sailor. "Etienne!"

He was even more shocked. "Mademoiselle Rostand!"

"Lock him up somewhere below," Longarm ordered. He turned to Jeanne, who hugged him.

"You are all right, Custis?"

"I'm fine," he assured her.

"What did you find out . . . about Maurice?"

"Accordin' to ol' Etienne there, your brother and Gullen and Shifflet have all headed inland, along with some men they hired to go with them."

She looked up at him and asked, "But why? Those mountains we saw when we arrived, they looked like a terrible place. What could be up there that is so important as to cause so much trouble?"

"I reckon we'll have to go and look," Longarm said.

Chapter 19

Captain Wood volunteered to go into town with them when Longarm and Jeanne went to talk to Leopardo, the hotel proprietor. Since Leopardo was an old friend, Wood thought the man would be more likely to cooperate if he was with them.

Longarm agreed. "We're obliged to you, Cap'n. This ain't your fight."

They went that night, when there would be fewer people around to notice them. Longarm was fairly certain Etienne had been telling him the truth about Rostand, Gullen, and Shifflet leaving San Ramon. The sailor had been too scared to lie. But Longarm hadn't survived as many years as he had in a highly dangerous profession without being cautious.

Captain Wood manned one of the oars in the little boat, one of his Cuban crewmen taking the other. When they reached shore, Wood left the Cuban to watch the boat while he, Longarm, and Jeanne went to the hotel.

"It's late," Longarm commented. "This fella Leopardo's liable to have gone to bed already."

"That's doubtful," the captain said. "He's usually got a poker game goin' in his office. I lost a considerable amount of money to him the last time I was here. That's how come I know he'll be glad to see me."

Longarm hoped Wood was right.

The furnishings in the hotel lobby were shabby but fairly clean. A skinny, slick-haired clerk greeted the captain with a toothy grin. "Ah, Capitan Wood!" he said. "I heard that the *Ozar* had docked in the harbor earlier today and was hoping that you would pay us a visit. Señor Leopardo is always glad to see you."

"Has he got a game goin' on tonight, Juan?" Wood asked.

The clerk shook his head. "No, capitan. But he is in his office going over the books. I will tell him you are here."

The man disappeared through a door at the end of the counter and came back a minute later still wearing the same grin. "Go right on back," he said. "You know the way, capitan."

Wood grunted and led the way down a short hall to a door that stood open. Inside was an office set on a corner of the building so there were windows on two sides and a little cross-ventilation. That helped in a hot, humid place like this, but not a whole lot. The thin, gauzy curtains over the open windows barely stirred in the gentle night breeze.

The man standing behind the desk in the office was stocky and middle-aged, with thinning gray hair and two balls of muscle that stood out on either side of his jaw as he grinned at them. He wore a white, lightweight suit and a white shirt with the collar unbuttoned.

"Capitan Wood," he said as he waved the visitors into the office. "So good to see you again. What can I do for you? Do your passengers wish accommodations?"

"Probably," Wood said. "We ain't discussed that. This here fella is Custis Long, and the lady is Mademoiselle Jeanne Rostand."

Longarm had told the captain not to reveal that he was a deputy U.S. marshal. They were going to play this hand a different way.

At the mention of Jeanne's name, Señor Leopardo's eyes

widened in recognition and surprise. He came out from
behind the desk and took her hand with Latin gallantry.

"Mademoiselle," he said. "Such an honor and a pleasure
to meet you. Would you by chance be related to M'sieu
Maurice Rostand, who was recently with us?"

"There is no chance about it, m'sieu," Jeanne said. "Maurice is my brother." She swallowed. "Is . . . is he here?"

Leopardo looked saddened. "Alas, no. He and his friends
left this very morning. They hired mules and men and set
out on an expedition into the mountains."

Longarm was thinking rapidly. He said, "Dang the luck.
I was afraid we had missed them. We were a couple of days
late gettin' here."

Leopardo frowned at him. "You were to meet M'sieu
Rostand and his party here? He said nothing about that."

Smiling, Jeanne said, "Ah, that is just like Maurice! So
absentminded he would forget to mention that his own sister was joining him. I was supposed to accompany him into
the mountains."

The hotel man's frown deepened. "Those mountains,
they are no place for a woman. Some call them the Devil's
Range, because of the smoke that rises from them at times.
The people say the mouth of Hell itself can be found up
there."

That was interesting, Longarm thought. The mountains
of Mexico were riddled with volcanoes, most of them dead.
Some of them were just dormant, though, and from time to
time the ground rumbled and shook, and smoke rose from
deep in the earth, emerging from those volcanic cones.
He'd had experiences of his own with Mexican volcanoes,
and Jessie Starbuck had told him once about how she had
survived the actual eruption of one, escaping the deadly
lava flow in a mad race on horseback down a mountainside.

Maybe whatever had led Rostand to the wilderness west
of the coastline had something to do with volcanoes, although Longarm still couldn't figure out what it might be.

"I will be fine," Jeanne assured Leopardo after the man
expressed his concern. She indicated Longarm with a ges-

ture of her small hand. "That is why M'sieu Long is with me. He is a most excellent bodyguard and traveling companion."

She was fast on her feet when it came to thinking. Longarm had to give her credit for that. They had talked about this and he had sketched in the basic approach they would take with Leopardo, but she was doing very well at filling in the details.

"Can you help us put together a party to go after M'sieu Rostand, Señor Leopardo?" Longarm asked. "We'll need mules and men, too. I hope the monsieur didn't hire all of them in town."

"No, no," Leopardo said with a wave of his hand. "Of course there are still men available. I will help you." He went to the door and called, "Juan! Come here, *por favor*."

Longarm figured Leopardo was going to send the desk clerk to start on the errand of rounding up men and mules for the trip into the mountains. They couldn't start tonight, of course, but Longarm wanted to be on the trail as early as he could the next morning. Rostand already had a day's lead on them, and it wasn't going to be easy following him into that rugged terrain.

Leopardo went back behind the desk. Juan's footsteps came down the hall. When the tall, skinny clerk stopped in the doorway, he held an old cap-and-ball pistol in both hands. The gun looked so heavy that it seemed Juan's thin arms would have trouble holding it up, but the barrel didn't waver even a fraction of an inch as he pointed the weapon at Longarm, Jeanne, and Captain Wood.

"Say!" the captain exclaimed. "What the hell is this all about?"

"My apologies, old friend," Leopardo said as he lifted a more modern Colt .45 from an open drawer of the desk and covered the three of them as well. "Unfortunately, even friendship has a price, and this hotel does not do as much business as it once did. I considered failing to honor the bargain I made, but in the end, I cannot."

"You . . . you . . ." Wood sputtered.

Longarm's jaw was clenched. Fear had appeared in
Jeanne's eyes. They had walked neatly into this trap. Rostand was an evil son of a bitch, but he was smart and had
prepared for any contingency. Assuming that he might be
followed, he had arranged with Leopardo to nab anybody
who showed up asking for him.

"What now?" Longarm asked. "You kill us and bury the
bodies in the forest or take them out in the Gulf and dump
them?"

"It would be an unforgiveable sin to harm a señorita as
lovely as Mademoiselle Rostand," Leopardo said. "She will
remain here in the hotel as my guest until M'sieu Rostand
and his friends return. As for Captain Wood . . . Valentine,
old amigo, you can return to your ship in the morning if
you give me your word you will weigh anchor, sail away
from San Ramon, and never speak of this matter to anyone."

Wood glared at him. "Damn it, you're puttin' me in one
hell of a bad spot here, Leopardo."

The hotel man shrugged. "It is your choice. Agree to
my suggestion, or you will suffer the same fate as Señor
Long . . . who is actually a lawman from the United States, I
believe." He looked at Longarm and shook his head. "Señor,
you have no legal right to be down here. I doubt you would
have told your superiors that you were breaking the law by
entering Mexico without authorization, so when you disap-
pear, no one will ever know what happened to you."

"I get it," Longarm drawled. "The girl lives, but I die."

Leopardo shrugged eloquently. "That is how M'sieu Rostand wished it, yes."

Longarm didn't believe in false modesty. He was mighty
fast on the draw, and he knew it. But with two guns already
drawn and aimed at him, there was no way he was fast
enough. If he reached for his Colt, he might get lead in both
Leopardo and Juan, but they would both shoot him. No
getting around it.

"No!" Jeanne cried out. "Whatever my brother paid you,
I will double it."

Leopardo shook his head. "M'sieu Rostand told me you would try such a tactic, mademoiselle, and that I was not to believe you, that you have no money of your own. He also told me to tell you that he will be glad to see you when he returns to San Ramon, because he assumes by then that you will have realized your place is with him."

Jeanne's lips drew back from her teeth in an angry snarl. "My brother can go to hell!" she spat. "I know now that I truly have no brother. He must be an imposter, because the brother I used to know could never be so evil!"

Leopardo smiled. "Perhaps you did not know him as well as you thought." He gestured with the gun. "Now, you and the captain will wait here with me. Juan, take Señor Long and deal with him."

"My pleasure," Juan said with that toothy grin of his.

This was actually a good development, Longarm thought rapidly. His chances of jumping Juan alone were much better.

Jeanne didn't let it come to that, though. Shouting a French curse, she whirled around suddenly and threw herself at the skinny clerk.

The boom of the old cap-and-ball pistol was deafeningly loud in the office. Longarm was moving even as Jeanne was, lunging across the desk and slashing the side of his hand into the wrist of Leopardo's gun hand. The .45 blasted, too, but Longarm had already knocked it aside before noise and flame spewed from the muzzle. Leopardo cried out in pain as the gun flew from his nerve-deadened fingers.

Longarm slid the rest of the way across the desk, scattering everything that was on it, and slammed into the hotel man. Leopardo went backward and landed in his chair, which overturned beneath him. Longarm heard a sharp crack which he took to be one of the chair legs breaking.

Leopardo gave a high, thin scream of pain, though. Longarm saw that the man's right arm was bent at an impossible angle. Leopardo had caught it somehow in the chair, and the bone had snapped when all of them went crashing to the floor. He might be in too much agony to care about the fight anymore, but Longarm made sure of that by hitting him so hard that Leopardo's head bounced off the floor with a thud. The hotel man went limp.

Longarm surged up, gun in hand. His head was full of fear for Jeanne. She had been practically on top of Juan when that old horse pistol went off. If she was hurt, he was going to blast that skinny son of a bitch straight to hell.

He saw that Jeanne was still on her feet, though, and Juan wasn't. The clerk was lying on the floor moaning as Captain Valentine Wood hit him again and again. Longarm spotted the cap-and-ball pistol in a corner where someone had kicked it.

He flung himself around the desk and grabbed Jeanne. "Are you all right?" he asked her, his eyes anxiously searching her body for any sign of a wound. He didn't see any bloodstains.

"What?" she said. Her voice sounded funny to him, muffled and far away, and he realized that his own voice had sounded that way, too. The gunshot had affected his hearing, and Jeanne had been even closer to the weapon when it went off. She might be completely deaf right now.

He raised his voice and asked, "Are you hurt?"

She either read his lips or made out some of the words, because she shook her head and said, "No. He missed me."

"Thank *El Señor Dios* for that," Longarm muttered. That was a damn fool stunt she had pulled, jumping Juan like that. But it appeared to have worked out.

Captain Wood got up off the now unconscious Juan. "I can't believe Leopardo would do that!" he said. "I just can't believe it."

"Like he said, even friendship has its price." Longarm stepped to the door and looked down the corridor toward the lobby. Nobody seemed to be coming to investigate the shot. He supposed the guests in the hotel and the citizens of San Ramon were smart enough to mind their own business.

Longarm shoved Juan's limp body aside with a foot and closed the door. He picked up the cap-and-ball pistol and handed it to Wood.

"Know how to use it?"

"Damn right I do," the captain growled. "I was in the Mexican War. Fought at Vera Cruz."

Longarm nodded. His hearing was getting back to normal now. "Keep an eye open for trouble."

"What are you gonna do?"

"Talk to Señor Leopardo," Longarm said.

He went behind the desk, set the chair upright, and hauled Leopardo up. The man was starting to come around, and he gasped in pain from his broken arm when Longarm shoved him down into the chair.

As Leopardo's eyelids started to flutter open, Longarm put his .44 in front of the man's face and let him get a good look at it.

"You need a doctor for that arm, old son," Longarm said. "I can see bone stickin' through the skin. You're liable to lose it if you don't get some attention."

"Help me," Leopardo moaned. "Please help me."

"Sure . . . but first you tell me the truth. Did Rostand and the others really go into the mountains?"

"*Sí.* They left . . . this morning . . . like I said." Leopardo had to force the words out between gritted teeth.

"Did they say where they were going? Exactly, I mean."

Sweat beaded Leopardo's face as the man shook his head. "N-no. Just . . . to the mountains. To the Devil's Range. It is the truth, I swear."

Something occurred to Longarm. "Did they have an old man with them?"

Leopardo swallowed and nodded. "Yes. He . . . he was a prisoner. I let them . . . keep him locked up in a storeroom."

Captain Wood made a disgusted sound. "You think you know a fella," he said.

Longarm ignored that. "Did they take the old man with them when they left?"

Leopardo nodded again, wordlessly this time.

So Rostand still had some use for old Gonzago, Longarm mused. The old man must have revealed some of what Rostand wanted to know, or else the Frenchman wouldn't have known to come here to San Ramon and take an expedition into the mountains. But Gonzago had to be holding something back, making himself still valuable to his captors. That was pretty smart.

"Did Rostand lay any more traps for us?" Longarm asked.

"I . . . I don't know. He paid me to watch for . . . his sister and a big American . . . who might be with her. I told Juan to . . . help me capture you. That is . . . all I know."

Longarm believed him. He glanced back at Wood and asked, "Do you know if there's a sawbones in this town, Captain?"

"Yeah. Had to have him stitch up one of my crewmen once while we were in port here. You want me to go to his house and bring him back?"

"Yeah. Reckon you can tie Juan up first, though?"

Wood grinned. "With pleasure. I'll even gag the son of a bitch, so he don't start yellin'."

When Wood had taken care of that chore and departed to find the doctor, Longarm asked Jeanne, "How are you hearin' now?"

"All right," she said. "There is a little ringing in my ears, but other than that I am fine."

"You're mighty lucky. That old horse pistol would've put a hole in you the size of a fist if Juan had hit you." He gestured toward a place where a chunk of plaster had been knocked out of the wall. "That's where the bullet landed."

Jeanne paled a little as she saw the damage. "Lucky indeed," she murmured. "But I could not allow these awful men to kill you, Custis."

"And I'm obliged to you for feelin' that way," he told her with a smile.

Wood came back with the doctor, a brisk little man with a brush of a mustache. He didn't seem to be thrown for a loop by what had happened here. His eyes had the world-weary look of most doctors who had seen just about everything, good and bad, that life on God's green earth had to offer.

The medico gave Leopardo something to knock him out,

then set the broken bone, cleaned the wound made by the jagged end, and splinted the arm. Longarm nodded toward the hotel man and said, "You can give him your bill in the mornin', Doc. We're all stayin' here tonight."

The doctor gave a stubborn shake of his head. "I cannot. There may be patients who have need of my services before morning."

Longarm frowned as he thought about that. The sawbones had a point.

"You give me your word on that oath you swore as a doctor that you won't say anything about this to anybody until after we're gone?"

"Of course," the doctor answered without hesitation. "I have long suspected that Señor Leopardo cheats at cards when I play with him. His fingers may not be so nimble when that broken arm heals."

Longarm couldn't help but chuckle at that. "All right, Doc. I'll take your word for it. Don't make me regret it, though."

The doctor nodded, took his medical bag, and went out.

Longarm thought about everything Leopardo had told him, and after a minute he said to Wood, "Do you happen to know where that storeroom is? The one where they kept the old man locked up?"

"Yeah, I do. Go on down the hall and through the door at the end."

"What is it, Custis?" Jeanne asked. "Why do you want to know about that?"

"Just a hunch," Longarm said. "I'm gonna go take a look."

"I will come with you."

He didn't try to stop her. Leaving Wood to keep an eye on Leopardo and Juan, they went down the hall and found the door to the storeroom. It was unlocked now that Gonzago wasn't being held prisoner in it anymore.

It was also dark and windowless. Longarm struck a lucifer and held the match up so that its glare filled the small room. Supplies filled the shelves on the walls, and crates and barrels filled about half the floor space. On the floor that was left lay a pile of blankets that had probably served as the old man's bed.

"What are you looking for?" Jeanne asked.

"I ain't quite sure. It's just that this is the closest we've been yet to old Gonzago, and I thought there might be somethin' . . ."

Other than the blankets, though, there was no sign that the man had ever been here. Grimacing in disgust, Longarm kicked the pallet aside.

Then caught his breath sharply and leaned over, holding the match close to the floor to reveal some marks that had been scratched into the boards somehow.

"What is that?" Jeanne asked as she leaned over to study the markings, too.

"Unless I miss my guess," Longarm said, "that's a map tellin' us how to get where we're goin'."

Chapter 20

Leopardo complained bitterly when he regained consciousness, but one hard look from Longarm shut him up. Maybe he realized that under the circumstances, he was lucky to be alive.

Longarm had fetched a piece of paper and a pencil from Leopardo's office and copied the angles and lines and twisting curves that Gonzago had scratched into the floor of his makeshift prison. When Longarm turned the paper a certain way, it was obvious that the pencil marks formed a map. He could make out the coastline, the small river that ran out of the mountains and emptied into the harbor, the rounded shapes of the hills, and then the jagged lines that represented the mountains. Another line ran along the course of the river, through the hills, and then angled up into the mountains through a gap between peaks that probably meant a pass.

From there, though, it ran straight to the top of one of the mountains deeper in the range, bisecting the angle of the marks that represented the mountain. Longarm wasn't sure what that meant, but he had a feeling they would have to climb that peak to find out.

Jeanne was exhausted. Longarm let her doze in an armchair in the corner of the office while he stood guard over

Leopardo and Juan. Captain Wood left, explaining that he would slip down to the harbor and tell his crewman to return to the ship.

"You might as well go back out to the *Ozar*, too, Cap'n," Longarm told him.

Wood shook his head. "No, I'm gonna stay here and help you round up that expedition. I know these folks better than you do, Marshal."

Longarm couldn't argue with that, so he thanked the captain for his help.

It was a long night, but dawn finally arrived. With it came a quiet knock on the office door. "It's me," Captain Wood called softly.

Longarm opened the door and was surprised to see not only the captain but also two of the three Cuban deckhands.

"We left Pasqual to watch the boat while we're gone," Wood explained as the men filed into the office. "Hector and Raul and me have decided we want to come with you."

"Into the mountains?" Longarm asked with a frown.

"Aye. It's true that we're seagoin' men, not landlubbers, but I got me a powerful curiosity about this whole affair. I want to see what's behind it. Hector and Raul just hope there'll be a fight at the end of it."

Longarm grunted. "I reckon I can practically guarantee that." The three men had brought rifles with them. "Are you any good with those guns?"

"Didn't I tell you I was in the Battle of Vera Cruz?"

"All right," Longarm shrugged. "You brought us down here, so I reckon you got a right to be in on the finish."

He already knew that he was going to have to take Jeanne with him. It wouldn't be safe to leave her here in San Ramon, not knowing who else Rostand might have paid off to help him. Longarm wanted them to get out of the settlement as fast as they could so they could take up the trail of their quarry.

That trail was going to follow the map Gonzago had left them. He was sure of it.

"I figure we need two or three other men, mules for

everybody, and three or four pack animals," Wood said. "Sound about right to you, Marshal?"

Longarm nodded. "You think you can find 'em?"

"Wait right here," Wood said confidently. "I'll be back as soon as I can."

Leopardo and Juan were both conscious now. Leopardo sat in the chair behind the desk while Juan was on the floor, propped up against a wall. The clerk was still tied and gagged.

Longarm moved to secure Leopardo into the chair with some cord he had found in the storage room. "You cannot leave us here like this," the hotel man said. "We will starve or die of thirst."

Longarm snorted. "The hell you will. Somebody will come along lookin' for you before the day is over. You'll be uncomfortable for a while, but you'll be all right. That's more than a back-stabbin' varmint like you deserves."

Even with a broken arm, Leopardo managed to shrug. "Each man does what he must," he said.

"Yeah, well, don't make me decide I must cut your throat before we leave."

Time passed slowly. The sun was up and climbing higher in the sky. Longarm knew Jeanne must be hungry. He certainly was. Neither of them had eaten since the night before, and right now they had no way of knowing when their next meal might be.

Not only that, but some of the hotel staff might show up at any time, looking for their boss. Longarm didn't want to take any more prisoners if he could avoid it.

It was about eight o'clock when Captain Wood returned. Longarm had gagged Leopardo by now. Wood had an eager grin on his whiskery face when Longarm opened the door to his quiet knock.

"Everybody's waiting out back," Wood reported as he jerked a thumb over his shoulder. "You ready to go?"

"More than ready," Longarm said. He ushered Jeanne out and didn't even look back at the two tied and gagged prisoners they were leaving behind them.

A rear door let them out into an alley behind the hotel. Three men Longarm had never seen before, along with Hector and Raul, waited on saddled mules. Each of the three Mexicans led a pack mule loaded with supplies.

There were three saddle mounts without riders. Longarm said to Jeanne, "I hope you don't mind ridin' a mule."

"I will be all right," she said. "I wish I was more suitably attired, though."

"Took care of that," Wood said. "Picked up a man's shirt and trousers the same place I got the provisions, ma'am. They were the smallest I could lay my hands on, so I hope they ain't too awful big."

Jeanne took the clothes he handed her and kissed him on the cheek. "*Merci*, Captain. We would be lost without you."

"Oh, I dunno about that," Wood said, blushing. "But I'm glad to do what I can to help."

Jeanne stepped back into the hotel for a moment to change. When she came out, she had the legs of the trousers and the sleeves of the shirt rolled up several turns each, and they were still a little big and baggy on her. They would be much better for riding into the mountains than her lightweight frock, though.

Longarm helped her get onto one of the mules, then swung up into the saddle of another.

"How'd you pay for this outfit?" he asked Wood.

"The mademoiselle told me where to find the money she had stashed in her cabin," the captain explained. "Don't worry, I just took what we needed."

"After all we've been through so far, I ain't worried about you turnin' into a petty thief, Cap'n." Longarm turned in the saddle to look back at the three Mexicans bringing up the rear of the procession. They all had the appearance of stolid peasants, probably either fisherman or farmers. "You reckon we can trust those fellas you hired to come with us?"

"If I didn't think so, I wouldn't have brung 'em," Wood said rather sharply.

Longarm grinned. "No offense. Just bein' careful."

"Well, I reckon you can't be too careful. But yeah, I trust

'em. I know all three of 'em. They've loaded and unloaded cargo on my ship plenty of times."

"You knew Leopardo, too," Longarm reminded him.

"Yeah, but not as well as I thought I did." Wood glanced at Jeanne and lowered his voice. "Seems to be a lot of that goin' around."

Longarm knew he was talking about Jeanne and her brother. The big lawman nodded.

They left San Ramon, cutting through back alleys until they reached the river. The stream wasn't very big, but it had a fairly strong current, flowing to the sea as it did from the heights of the mountains. A path ran alongside, with the river to the right and the forest bulking thickly to the left. Sometime in the past, the people of this area had hacked out this passage to make it possible to follow the river inland.

Hector took the lead, carrying his rifle across his saddle in front of him. He was a keen-eyed young man, and Longarm figured he would spot any danger that approached them. He rode next, followed by Jeanne and then Captain Wood. The three Mexicans with the pack mules followed the captain, and Raul brought up the rear, keeping an eye on their back trail.

It didn't take long to pass through the mile or so of forest that lined the coast. The band of hills was considerably wider. Hours rolled by while the riders steadily made their way west, away from the Gulf of Mexico.

Longarm glanced back from time to time and thought about Leopardo and Juan. He figured either someone had found them or they had gotten free on their own by now. He had to wonder if Leopardo would send men after them to seek vengeance for that broken arm. Longarm didn't think that was too likely. The hotel man struck him as too mercenary for that. Leopardo would take money to kill, but Longarm doubted if he would pay others to kill for him.

Still, he would be alert for trouble coming up behind them, even though he figured the real danger was somewhere up ahead in the mountains that loomed against the blue sky, seemingly close enough to touch even though they were still miles and miles away.

They stopped at midday to rest the mules and make a quick lunch from the supplies they had brought along with them. The food was simple but tasted delicious to Longarm. They had full canteens, but he washed the meal down with water from the river, which was cold and clear, although it had a faintly sulphurous odor and taste to it. That was because it came from springs in those volcanic peaks, he thought.

After pushing on all afternoon, they still hadn't reached the end of the hills when night fell. They made camp next to the river. Longarm spoke Spanish very well, so he asked the men who had come with them from San Ramon how long it would take to reach the mountains.

When Jeanne asked him what they said, he told her, "They claim it'll take at least a couple more days to make it through the foothills. I didn't show them the map, so they don't know exactly where we're goin', but I'll bet we're talkin' another day or so to reach that pass, and once we're beyond it, maybe a couple of days to the top of the mountain."

Jeanne gave a low moan of dismay and said, "Five more days of riding these . . . these beasts?" She rubbed her aching backside.

Longarm smiled. "At least five days," he corrected her. "And a lot of times, a mule's actually easier ridin' than a horse. We're lucky to have 'em."

They pitched tents to help keep the insects at bay, although Longarm knew that some of the little biting critters would still reach them. Jeanne insisted on sharing a tent with him. She asked him to massage the muscles of her inner thighs that were so sore from riding all day. Longarm complied, and he wasn't a bit surprised when she took hold of his head and urged him down between her widespread legs. He spread her open with his thumbs, licking her from one of her openings to the other, then speared his tongue inside her and soon brought her to climax.

She dozed off before she could return the favor, but Longarm didn't mind too much. She'd had a long, hard day, after all. For a pampered French gal who had led a life of ease and luxury until now, she was doing just fine, he thought.

The next day, the hills became steeper and more rugged, becoming foothills for the mountains known unofficially as Sierra Diablo, the Devil's Range. The journey wasn't much more difficult, though, because the river still wound between the hills and the trail followed it.

Things wouldn't stay that way, Longarm knew. In another day or so, if old Gonzago's map was right, the stream would curve away to the north, but their route would continue on straight into the mountains.

That night, Jeanne insisted that she pleasure him first, since she had gone to sleep the night before. Longarm never argued with a beautiful woman who wanted to suck his cock—well, not very often, anyway—and with Jeanne's skills, it wasn't long before he was exploding in her mouth, causing her to swallow eagerly.

The map was sort of shy on landmarks, but it had enough so Longarm was pretty sure the next day that they had reached the spot where they were supposed to turn away from the river, which had already started its great northward curve.

"How do you suppose Gonzago knew what to put on the map?" Jeanne asked as she rode alongside Longarm. "Do you think he has been over this route before?"

"Maybe," Longarm said. "Or maybe he was just going by what he read on the back of the Star of Father Cristobal."

"The relic!" Jeanne exclaimed. "Of course. The directions to wherever we are going were written on it."

"In a language the priests couldn't understand," Longarm reminded her.

"What do you think it might be?"

A faint inkling had started to drift around in the back of Longarm's mind, but he was a long way from sure about anything yet. Preferring to keep the speculation to himself, he just shook his head and said, "Farther along we'll know more about it, to quote the old hymn."

The going was much tougher once they veered away from the stream. The terrain became rougher and more arid, and the sun beat down on them with increasing force. Longarm could tell it was hard on Jeanne, and on Captain Valentine Wood as well. The captain, tough as nails though he might be, was probably a little too old for such a rugged journey.

Wood didn't complain, though, and neither did Jeanne.

By late in the afternoon, they had reached the base of the long slope that led up to the pass marking the real gateway into the mountains. Although there was still some daylight left, Longarm knew that all of them needed to be fresh when they started making that climb, so he called a halt.

"We'll camp here," he said, "and start up in the mornin'."

He had gotten worried that someone in Rostand's party might have spotted them from a vantage point up there in those rearing heights. Rostand had been careful every step of the way so far, and Longarm didn't expect him to stop now. The big lawman split up guard shifts among the men.

The night passed quietly and peacefully. In the morning, they began the long ascent to the pass. It would take them most of the day to get there, Longarm knew. They would camp either in the pass or just beyond it.

More than ever that day, he was glad they were mounted on strong, sure-footed mules. The beasts never seemed to tire, and they were good at picking their way along the narrow trail that zigzagged its way up the side of the mountain. At times they were on fairly solid ground, but at other times the slope was steep and hundreds of feet of open air yawned all too closely to one side or the other.

Longarm could tell from Jeanne's pale, drawn face that she was frightened, and he didn't blame her. They had come too far to turn back now, though, so they pushed on, sometimes dismounting to lead the mules.

Late in the day, they reached the top of the pass without mishap. Two mountains came together here, gray, shouldering peaks that rose several hundred feet higher on each side of the gap, which was no more than twenty feet wide. It ran for about a quarter of a mile between the mountains. The sides of the passage were littered with boulders that had tumbled down from above during the passing centuries.

Longarm led the way through the pass and called a halt. He leaned forward in the saddle to ease aching muscles, then motioned for Jeanne to come up beside him. She had grown stronger and tougher, and the riding didn't bother her as much now, but she still heaved a sigh of relief as she reined in. Then she looked out in front of them and said softly, "Oh."

The landscape dropped down in spectacular fashion, stretching for miles in a stark panorama mostly composed of browns, grays, and tans but streaked through here and there with red and gold and black. Across the valley, another mountain reared even higher and more rugged than the ones that surrounded them now. With the late afternoon sunlight behind it, it loomed dark and sinister like some prehistoric monster, and the plumes of smoke curling from its summit, like smoke from the snout of a dragon, reinforced that image.

"Is that where we are going?" Jeanne asked in a hushed voice.

"I reckon it is," Longarm replied.

And then another voice, loud and harsh and edged with cruelty, said, "It damn sure is."

Longarm jerked around in the saddle to see Joshua Gullen standing at the side of the pass pointing a rifle at a shaken-looking Captain Valentine Wood. Gullen wasn't alone, either. Shifflet and several other men had stepped out from behind the boulders where they had been hiding, and the rifles in their hands covered the rest of the party.

"Well, well," Gullen said as he leered at Jeanne. "I'll bet Rostand's gonna be damn glad to see his little sis again. I know I am."

Chapter 21

Longarm felt anger boiling up inside him, most of it directed at himself. Gullen and his men had laid a good trap. They had been so well hidden inside the pass that Longarm hadn't seen them, even though he had been alert for that very thing.

He had known from the start that once they approached the mountains, Rostand's party might look back and spot them. There had been no way of avoiding that danger, though. They'd had to follow the only map they had been given.

Anyway, they had to catch up to the varmints sooner or later, he told himself. He would have preferred doing it on his own terms, rather than as prisoners, but . . .

"Take it easy with that rifle, old son," he told Gullen. "Don't go gettin' an itchy trigger finger."

"Oh, it's itchy, all right," the killer said. "It's itchin' to blow you right outta that saddle, Long. That's the only way we can be sure you won't give us any more trouble."

Longarm snorted. "Do that and you're gonna be in more trouble than you know. Rostand won't be happy when he gets back to San Ramon and finds out that he don't have a yacht anymore."

He saw Jeanne's eyes cut toward him and hoped she

would play along with the ruse he had come up with. She'd been good about that so far.

Gullen lowered the barrel of his rifle a little and frowned. "What the hell are you talkin' about? What's wrong with the *Bellefleur*?"

"Nothin' . . . so far. But Cap'n Wood and his men boarded it and took it over when we got to San Ramon. We left some of 'em on there with a box of dynamite, and if they don't see me and the cap'n and the rest of his crew when you ride up, they'll blow that fancy yacht to kindlin'."

Gullen's lip curled in a sneer. "You're a fuckin' liar."

"Kill us and see," Longarm said with a shrug. "If you're wrong, Rostand's gonna be stuck in that piss-poor little town until some other seagoin' vessel happens to come along. Who knows how long that will be?"

Doubt had entered Gullen's eyes, Longarm saw as the man strode closer. "Rostand told us to kill everybody except his sister."

"Hell, man, what do you think we're doin'?" Longarm demanded. "We didn't come all the way up here in these mountains for our health. We're bringin' the little slut to him!"

"Custis!" Jeanne gasped. Longarm couldn't tell if she was acting or if she was really shocked. Either way, it was just the reaction he'd hoped for.

He looked over at her and said, "Sorry, darlin'. I know you're powerful mad at your brother, but I'm givin' you back to him and throwin' in with him. Why do you think I came down here to Mexico in the first place? I don't have any jurisdiction on this side of the border. I want a share of whatever he's after, and I ain't ever goin' back."

"That's a likely story," Gullen said. "You came down here to square accounts with me for killin' that dancer in San Antonio."

Longarm laughed. "Travel hundreds of miles and risk my life because some Mex whore got herself killed? Old son, you don't know me at all. I don't give a damn about that. I've been after a piece of this game right from the start.

Who wouldn't be? We're talkin' about a fuckin' silver star
with diamonds and emeralds and rubies on it!"

"We're talkin' about a lot more than that," Gullen muttered, but he didn't elaborate. He still didn't look convinced
that Longarm was telling the truth, not by a long shot, but
Longarm had never figured that he could get the hired killer
to swallow the story whole. All he wanted to do was create
enough doubt in Gullen's mind that the man would hold off
on killing him and Wood and the others for the time being.

It appeared that he might have been successful in that.

Or maybe not, because Gullen abruptly raised the rifle
again and centered his sights on Longarm. The big lawman
was about to make a desperate grab for his Colt and dive
out of the saddle when Gullen snapped an order.

"Drop your guns. All of you!"

Gullen wouldn't bother disarming them, not if he was
going to murder them out of hand.

"We'll let Rostand sort all this out," Gullen went on.

Shifflet frowned. "Boss, are you sure that's a good idea?"
he asked. "The French said to kill 'em all. He didn't make
no bones about it."

Gullen said, "I don't want to take a chance on that boat
gettin' blown up. Long's smart enough and stubborn enough
to do just that."

And he might have attempted it, Longarm mused, if he
had thought about it before they left San Ramon. On the
other hand, a lie was as good as the truth as long as folks
believed it. The politicians in Washington proved that every
day. And he hadn't had a big enough force to capture the
Bellefleur, anyway.

Gullen didn't know that, though.

"I said to drop those guns," Gullen barked. "Do it now,
before I change my mind."

Longarm knew that surrendering was a calculated risk.
But it would keep them alive and get them to where they
wanted to go anyway. They could deal with the problem of
being unarmed later.

Using his left hand, he slid the Colt from its holster,

leaned over, and dropped it on the ground. Captain Wood, Hector, Raul, and the Mexicans all threw down their rifles.

"What about the girl?" Gullen asked.

Jeanne gave him a haughty glare. "I do not carry a gun, M'sieu Gullen."

"You better be tellin' the truth. If I suspect you ain't, I'll have to search you." A leer made the gunman's ugly face even uglier. "I might just do it anyway. From what I hear about how randy you are, I don't figure you'd mind too much."

"Be careful," she told him coldly. "I will be back with my brother soon, and you will treat me with respect."

"Sure, sure." Gullen's men had gathered up the guns. "Let's go."

They prodded the prisoners down the slope. The mules used by Gullen and his men were hidden in a brushy thicket several hundred yards below the pass. They picked the animals up and continued on.

With Gullen riding beside them, gun in hand, Longarm looked over at Jeanne and said, "I'm sorry about what you heard back there. Figured it was time you knew the truth, though."

Angry French words lashed at him. "I cannot believe I ever trusted you, you . . . you . . ."

She finished with another French epithet. He hoped it was suitably nasty, just in case any of their captors spoke the language. If they believed she was really mad at him, it would help keep them alive a little longer.

With night coming on, they couldn't go very far. The trail wound around a rocky ridge and came to a shoulder of ground that wasn't visible from above. A camp was set up there, with a number of tents and a makeshift rope corral.

Maurice Rostand emerged from one of the tents. He must have heard the hoofbeats of the approaching mules. The Frenchman wore lace-up boots, canvas trousers, a work shirt, and a planter's hat of cream-colored felt. He strode toward the newcomers as they reined in.

"Jeanne!" Rostand said. "Jeanne, my dear sister! It's so good to see you again. Are you all right?"

She regarded him coldly from the back of her mule. "You deserted me, Maurice," she said. "You have no right to inquire as to my health."

"I always planned to come back for you," he said, looking offended. "I would not abandon my own flesh and blood."

"You ordered your men to shoot at me! You didn't care if I was killed!"

"They were shooting at Marshal Long. Anyway, I knew he would protect you."

Jeanne said, "Oh! How little you know!"

Gullen chuckled, too, causing Rostand to frown in confusion. "What is going on here?" he demanded.

Gullen jerked a thumb toward Longarm. "The lawdog here says he wants to throw in with you. Says he brought your sister along just so he could give her back to you."

Rostand gave a snort of disbelief. "And you think he was telling the truth? I wondered why you brought them here. I told you to kill everyone except Jeanne." He didn't sound happy that Gullen hadn't followed that order.

"That ain't all," the gunman said. "He claims they took over the *Bellefleur* and planted dynamite on it. He says that if they ain't with us when we get back to San Ramon, the men they left behind will blow up the ship."

Rostand waved a hand. "Patently, another lie."

"Probably, but we can't be sure. I don't know about you, but I don't want to be stuck in some backwater Mexican village. My share of that fortune won't do me much good there."

Rostand's mouth tightened at Gullen's mention of a fortune. Gullen hadn't really spilled anything Longarm hadn't guessed already, though. He still didn't know the details, but he knew Rostand wouldn't have gone to so much trouble unless there was going to be a big payoff at the end.

"All right. We'll keep them alive . . . for now. Watch

them closely, though. If there is any trouble, I will hold you responsible, Gullen."

The killer grunted. "Fine by me. This bunch ain't gonna be able to do a damn thing to stop us from gettin' what we're after. We're too close now."

"Yes," Rostand agreed. He turned his head to look toward the top of the mountain looming over them. "It all depends on how long it takes us to reach the city." He stepped over to Jeanne's mule and held a hand up to her. "Come with me. You can be comfortable in my tent."

She glared down at him for a moment, then shrugged and relented. "It *is* good to see you again, Maurice," she said. "Just one thing first."

She turned in the saddle, reached out, and slapped Longarm hard. Her hand made a sharp crack as it struck his face and jerked his head to the side. She spat another French curse at him.

"He is a terrible, horrible American brute, Maurice," she said, letting a tear trickle down her cheek as she allowed her brother to help her dismount. "I cannot begin to tell you how awful it has been being with him."

"Do not worry," he told her. "You are back where you belong now." He put an arm around her shoulders. "Come with me."

As they walked off toward Rostand's tent, Gullen gestured with his gun at the prisoners. "The rest of you get down."

They dismounted. Gullen ordered his men to tie them up, except for Longarm. He marched the big lawman at gunpoint over to one of the other tents.

"You got special accommodations for me?" Longarm asked dryly.

"There's somebody in there I figured you might want to meet," Gullen said. "Go on in."

Longarm pushed aside the canvas flap over the tent's entrance, bent over, and stepped in. There was still enough light for him to be able to make out a figure sitting crosslegged on the ground. The man lifted his head, and Longarm saw an old, weathered face the color of saddle leather. The man had thinning, snow-white hair and a short beard of the same color. He wore peasant garb: rope-soled sandals, white, pajama-like trousers and shirt, and a woven serape. Longarm knew he was looking at the man he had come all this way to find.

Gonzago.

Chapter 22

"Señor?" the old man muttered wearily.

Gullen laughed. "I thought you might like to see the man who came to save you and that precious relic of yours. He's a prisoner just like you are. You can see now there ain't no hope for you, *viejo*. You might as well cooperate and give Rostand what he wants."

"I have brought him this far, have I not?" Gonzago asked.

"Yeah, and somehow you left a clue for this damn lawman to find, or else he wouldn't be here. And you haven't told the Frenchman everything he wants to know, either." Gullen gave Longarm a hard shove that sent him to the ground. "But you will, now that you realize there ain't nobody gonna come and rescue you. Might as well tell Rostand what he wants to know. Maybe he'll let you live."

Longarm knew how unlikely that was, and from the look of resignation in Gonzago's eyes, the old man knew, too.

"There'll be at least two guards outside this tent all the time," Gullen went on. "Rostand ain't decided what to do with you yet, Long, but if you give any trouble, we'll save him the trouble and just kill you. Savvy?"

"Yeah," Longarm said. "I savvy."

Gullen ducked back out of the tent. Longarm was left alone with the old man.

Gonzago wasn't tied up, but where was there for him to go in this rugged wilderness? He wouldn't survive for long, on foot and with no supplies. He had to know that, therefore he wasn't trying to escape.

Things looked almost that bad for Longarm and his friends. Rostand definitely had the upper hand . . . for now.

Meanwhile, Longarm finally had a chance to find out what this was all about.

He leaned forward and pitched his voice low as he said in Spanish, "Gonzago, I'm Deputy U.S. Marshal Custis Long. I've come to rescue you and recover the Star of Father Cristobal."

Gonzago laughed humorlessly. "How can you help me? You are a prisoner, too."

"Yeah, but I don't plan on stayin' that way. I figured I'd let Rostand take us the rest of the way to the lost city, and then make my move."

Gonzago's head came up sharply in surprise. "You know of the lost city?" he asked.

"I made a guess," Longarm said, "based on somethin' Rostand said a little while ago. He mentioned a city on top of that mountain, and I've seen enough maps of Mexico to know there's not a city up there that anybody knows about today, so it must be lost. My other hunch is that it was built by the ancient Aztecs."

Gonzago leaned forward eagerly and said, "Yes! That is what is written on the Star. It tells how to find the city of Nahu-Alatl."

"Written in the Aztec language?"

Gonzago nodded. "Yes. The high priest of Nahu-Alatl taught it to Fray Cristobal while he was there."

"Hold it," Longarm said. "Back up a mite. How come you can read that ancient tongue?"

"You would not know it to see me driving a produce cart, but I was once a professor of antiquities at the university in Mexico City. Then my wife and my children all died of a fever, and I could no longer stand to stay in that place. So I came north to live with relatives in San Antonio. I put

my old life behind me. This was many years ago, but the
knowledge I had then is still in my head now."

Longarm nodded. "All right, I reckon that makes sense.
But what was that about Father Cristobal bein' in this city
of . . . what did you call it?"

"Nahu-Alatl," Gonzago said. "It was an outpost of the
Aztec Empire before Cortes came from Spain and left it
shattered. And it survived long after the rest of the empire
had fallen, so that the priests there could carry out their
sacred duty and protect the Treasure of the Sun." Warming
to his subject like the teacher he had once been, the old
man went on, "You see, Marshal Long, for many years the
leaders of the Aztecs secreted much of their wealth in
Nahu-Alatl. The Spaniards looted much wealth from the
empire, but there was even more hidden away which they
did not know about."

Longarm frowned in thought. "So when Father Cristobal
was lost and tryin' to make it to San Antonio, he stumbled
onto this place?"

Gonzago nodded. "Yes, and the high priest cared for him,
saving his life."

"So that was the miracle the old padre talked about,"
Longarm murmured.

"Yes. Fray Cristobal claimed to have followed a star to
Nahu-Alatl, and that gave him the idea to make an icon in
honor of his salvation, once he finally reached San Antonio.
He even had the jewels with which to decorate it."

"He brought them with him from the Aztec city," Longarm said as understanding came to him.

Once again the old man nodded. "Yes, the priest gave
them to him. The wealth of those jewels represents only the
tiniest fraction of what is still there in Nahu-Alatl."

Longarm frowned. "But it was the priest's duty to protect the old Aztec treasure. Why would he give some of it
away to a priest from a different religion?"

"Because Fray Cristobal agreed to preserve the story of
Nahu-Alatl. You see, by the time he found the city, all the
inhabitants had died out except for the old high priest. He

was the last of the true Aztecs, and he knew his time to leave this world was upon him. He nursed Fray Cristobal back to health, and then Fray Cristobal remained in the city until the high priest passed away. Even in his aged infirmity, the high priest had faithfully tended the gardens, so there was food for Fray Cristobal to take with him, and that helped him to make his way at last to Texas."

Longarm's eyes narrowed as he studied the old man's face in the gathering darkness inside the tent. He said, "No offense, Gonzago, but I know good and well nobody could write down this whole story on the back of a silver star. How'd you learn all of it?"

Gonzago chuckled. "You believe I am lying?"

"I didn't say that."

"The story of Fray Cristobal's visit to Nahu-Alatl is not written on the back of the Star. Only the directions for how to find the city. The rest of it he wrote in a manuscript that I found in the archives of Mission San Jose several years ago. It had been gathering dust for decades because no one there could read it."

"Because Father Cristobal wrote it in the Aztec language."

"That is right. You see, Marshal Long, the padre promised to preserve the memory of Nahu-Alatl, but at the same time, he wanted to protect the city." A bitter edge came into the old man's voice. "He did not want it looted by men such as Rostand."

"How in the world did he find out about the lost city and its connection to the Star?"

"When the Emperor Maximilian ruled Mexico some years ago, one of Rostand's cousins was a high-ranking member of the imperial court in Mexico City. Somehow he heard about the old legend of a lost Aztec city where a great treasure could be found. In his greed to find out more, he hired scholars to dig into the legend, and they uncovered the possibility that Fray Cristobal might have traveled through the area where the city was rumored to be located. He dispatched spies to San Antonio, who sent back word of the

silver star Fray Cristobal had made, with the writing on it
that no one could read. Thinking that there might be a connection, Rostand's cousin would have paid his agents to
steal the Star then, but before he could do that, Maximilian
was overthrown and the man was killed in the fighting. Not
before he had written everything in a letter to Rostand's
father, however. But the elder Rostand, who was already
rich, did not attempt to find out more about the Treasure of
the Sun. Eventually he died and that letter was passed down
to Maurice Rostand."

"Who wants the treasure for himself even though he's
already got a boatload of money," Longarm said.

"Unfortunately, yes. The man is a monster of avarice,
always wanting more and more, no matter how much he
already has. I think it is more a matter of power and ambi-
tion than actual wealth."

"Yeah, some hombres are like that," Longarm said. "So
he came to San Antonio and paid some varmints to steal the
Star."

With a note of amusement in his voice again, Gonzago
said, "Yes, and then he was arrogant enough to think that he
could translate the writing on it himself. He fancies himself
a scholar, you see, but in reality he is just a greedy fool. He
struggled with the writing for more than a week."

"Then he gave up and had you kidnapped, because
somebody at the mission told him you claimed you could
read what was on the Star. I happened to come along about
the same time, because my boss wanted me to find the Star
and keep the peace between my government and the Mexicans."

"I would say that fate led you there," Gonzago replied.
"It is now your destiny to be the protector of Nahu-Alatl
and the Treasure of the Sun, Marshal Long. Legend fore-
tells that such a hero will always arise in times of need."

Longarm drew back a little and said, "Hold on there, old
son. I'm just a lawman. I ain't no Aztec hero. I just want to
see justice done."

"And justice means not allowing Rostand and his allies

to loot the treasure of a once proud and noble people."

Longarm tugged at his earlobe. "Well, you might have somethin' there," he admitted. "I want to return that Star to the mission where it belongs, and I want Rostand and Gullen to pay for the death of an innocent young woman. I reckon to do that, I'll have to play hob with their plans."

"And how do you intend to do that while you are a prisoner?"

"That's the part I ain't figured out yet," Longarm said. "But I'm workin' on it."

Chapter 23

A while later, one of the guards brought them a meager meal of beans and tortillas. After they had eaten, Gonzago dozed off, but Longarm lay awake for a long time, thinking about what the old man had told him.

It was a fantastic story, and he wasn't sure he believed all of it, although Gonzago had certainly seemed sincere. And Rostand believed it, which had been enough to set off a long chain of violence.

Eventually, Longarm dozed off, and when he woke up the next morning, he wasn't any closer to coming up with a way of turning the tables on their captors. For the time being, he would play along and wait until they reached the lost city before he made his move. Circumstances might have changed by then.

They had beans and tortillas again for breakfast, then the prisoners were herded to their mules and forced to mount up. Longarm was relieved to see that Captain Wood, Hector, and Raul all appeared to be unharmed, along with the three Mexicans who had come with them from San Ramon. The hired men were frightened, no doubt, but the captain and the two Cuban sailors all still had looks of defiance in their eyes.

Longarm hoped they wouldn't try anything before the

expedition reached its destination. He wanted as many allies as possible when he struck back against Rostand and Gullen.

Jeanne came out of her brother's tent with Rostand. She seemed to be all right, too. She gave him a quick, haughty look, as if she were still angry with him, and then turned her face away from him, but in that brief glimpse Longarm thought he had seen fear in her eyes. That told him she hadn't really gone back over to her brother's side. She was just playing along with Rostand.

He helped her mount, then swung up into the saddle himself. With a smile, he brought his mule alongside Longarm's and said, "I suppose you and the old man had a nice long talk, Marshal. You know about the Treasure of the Sun now, do you not?"

Longarm didn't see any point in denying it. "Sounds like quite a passel of loot," he said. "There ought to be plenty to go around, Rostand."

"And you really think I will give you a share and allow you to live simply because you returned my sister to me?" Rostand laughed. "Well, who knows? I might be feeling generous once we get back to San Ramon. But I would not count on it, Marshal."

Longarm didn't show the satisfaction he felt at the veiled hint Rostand intended to keep him alive until they returned to the seacoast town. The Frenchman believed that story about blowing up the *Bellefleur* just enough to be cautious.

The expedition set off, descending deeper into the valley and then starting the ascent again, this time climbing toward the summit of the mountain where the lost city of Nahu-Alatl was supposed to be located. As they rode, Longarm looked up at the peak and again saw tendrils of smoke or steam rising from the summit.

After his previous encounter with a volcano, he had done some reading up on the things at the Denver Public Library. A volcano could go hundreds of years between eruptions. During those intervals, time and nature sometimes formed a flat plug in the opening where molten lava and noxious gases had once streamed out. That caldera, as it was called, might seem stable, and it could remain that way over many lifetimes.

Could those ancient Aztecs have really built their outpost in the caldera of a dormant volcano? It seemed to Longarm like a damn fool thing to do, but maybe they hadn't realized what they were sitting on top of.

The serpentine trail crawled up the side of the mountain, reaching even more dizzying heights than the one on the other side of the pass. The climb, hard as it was, didn't take as much time as Longarm thought it might. He had expected them to have to spend one more night on the trail, but late that afternoon, a bone-weary bunch of mules and riders neared the top of the mountain.

During the day, Jeanne had ignored him. That was all right with Longarm. Let her keep playing her part for now. He had managed to talk quietly again with Gonzago, and the old man admitted that he had translated enough of the writing on the Star to allow them to get this far.

"The one called Gullen beat me," Gonzago said. "And Rostand threatened worse tortures. I am an old man. I am not as strong as I once was."

"And deep down, you want to see this place for yourself, don't you?" Longarm asked.

Gonzago looked like he wanted to deny it, but then he shrugged and said, "After reading Fray Cristobal's story, to be able to lay eyes on such a fabulous place . . . Such opportunities do not come to every man, Marshal."

"No, they don't," Longarm had agreed. He was sort of eager to see Nahu-Alatl himself.

Now he was on the verge of doing just that. As the riders halted, Shifflet came back and motioned to Longarm. "Rostand wants you and the old man up ahead."

They rode to the front of the party. Rostand, Jeanne, and Gullen had stopped at the forward edge of a broad, flat piece of ground. As Longarm and Gonzago moved up closer, Longarm saw the ground dropping away and opening up in front of them. His breath hissed between his teeth as he came up far enough to see the whole thing.

Just as he had suspected, the old volcano had formed a caldera. It was a depression several hundred feet deep and maybe two miles across, ringed by the jagged edge of the volcano's crater. This one trail was the only easy way in and out. Maybe the only way, period, considering how rugged those crater walls were.

The trail descended a fairly easy slope and turned into a broad avenue that had once been paved with flagstones. Over time, those stones had eroded, but from up here it was still easy to see the road. It was lined with the weathered remains of dozens of flat-topped pyramids, the homes of the ancient Aztec nobility. Other pyramids were scattered around the caldera, including one off to the side that rose to a conical top. That was probably a temple of some sort, Longarm thought. There were also a number of more conventional-looking adobe structures, probably where the slaves and the commoners had lived.

"Nahu-Alatl," Gonzago breathed in awe. "It really exists."

Rostand looked over at him. "Did you think it did not, old man?"

"I hoped it was real . . . but I could never be sure, not until I saw it with my own eyes."

"I feel the same way about the Treasure of the Sun," Rostand said. "Now, you have denied me the final piece of the puzzle long enough. Where is it?"

Gonzago pointed at the huge, cone-shaped pyramid. "In there. The Temple of the Sun God."

Rostand hitched his horse into motion. "Come on," he ordered. "I don't want to waste any time."

He led the way down the slope toward the old boulevard.

Longarm looked around the ancient, ruined city and saw what looked like smoke rising in several places. But it wasn't smoke, he knew, but rather steam escaping from vents in the earth. He had seen similar things up in the Yellowstone country.

"You know this place is sittin' right on top of a damn volcano, don't you?" he asked Rostand.

"A dormant volcano," the Frenchman replied. "We are in no danger from it."

"See that steam comin' up? It don't look so dormant to me."

"We won't be here long," Rostand snapped. "We'll find the treasure, load it, and leave."

"You can't get back down the mountain today," Longarm pointed out. "Even if you camp outside the crater, you'll still be practically on top of the thing."

"What's he talkin' about?" Gullen demanded. "You didn't say anything about some volcano erupting, Rostand."

With growing frustration in his voice, Rostand said, "It's not going to erupt! We're perfectly safe. This city was built more than five hundred years ago, and you can see that most of the buildings are still standing."

"Yeah, but I've heard about volcanoes. They can blow their tops just about any time, can't they?"

"If you are frightened, you can leave," Rostand said coldly. "As for me, I am going to find a fortune in gold and gems."

"Take it easy," Gullen said. "I didn't say I was goin' anywhere. I just don't like it here very much, that's all."

"Neither do I," said Longarm. "You ever stop to think about how many old Aztec ghosts must be roamin' around this place?"

Rostand snorted. "Ghosts!" he repeated. "Do not even attempt such a transparent ploy, Marshal. You are not going to frighten my men into fleeing. They have been well paid, and they are loyal to me."

Longarm wasn't so sure about that. When he glanced at the Mexicans who had come along with Rostand, they looked mighty nervous. So did the ones Captain Wood had hired, for that matter. And the captain, Hector, and Raul weren't exactly relaxed, either. As the riders started up the long boulevard between the ancient buildings, a definite air of tension hung over the entire group. The fact that the sun would be down soon and it would be growing dark didn't help matters.

"A city of the dead," Longarm muttered, loud enough for those close by him to hear. He heard mutters spreading in Spanish through the men behind him.

Jeanne said, "Maurice, perhaps we should leave and come back tomorrow."

"Nonsense," he answered without hesitation. "I brought along plenty of torches. I want to find that treasure."

Longarm said, "I always figured no treasure was worth my life."

Rostand's head jerked toward him. "Quiet!"

Gullen said, "All right, I don't like this. I'm as interested in loot as the next fella, but it can wait until tomorrow, Rostand."

"Yeah, this damn place gives me the fantods," Shifflet agreed.

"I told you, go if you wish. I will claim all the treasure as my own," Rostand said.

"The hell with that," Gullen said angrily.

Longarm said, "I just saw somebody run around that pyramid over yonder."

They all jerked their heads around to look where he was pointing. The weathered old pyramid seemed deserted in the fading light.

The weird thing was, Longarm wasn't lying. He really *had* seen something dart around the pyramid. The next second, Shifflet let out a howl and pointed in the other direction. "There's one over there, too!"

Everybody was looking around now. The men who were armed clutched their rifles and looked like they were ready to start blazing away. Longarm twisted in the saddle and spotted two more of the shadowy shapes.

Suddenly, Shifflet screamed, "Aztec ghosts!" and flung his rifle to his shoulder. He started cranking off rounds as fast as he could work the Winchester's lever. He had blasted a handful of rounds, firing wildly, when he pitched forward out of his saddle and landed face down on the ground. An arrow protruded from his back.

Ghosts, hell! Longarm thought.

They were being attacked by Indians.

That came as no real surprise. Longarm had run into Yaqui Indians in northern Mexico on several occasions, and the Yaquis had plenty of almost equally savage cousins farther south. Some of them must have decided to settle in this long-lost city, and they didn't like it when invaders came riding in. Some of them might have never even seen a white man before, let alone a woman with auburn hair like Jeanne.

More arrows came flying out from the places where the archers had taken cover. More shots slammed out and echoed from the walls of the crater as the members of the expedition fought back.

"The temple!" Rostand shouted. "We can hold them off there!"

Longarm wasn't sure about that, but it was the closest place they might find some decent cover. He wasn't going there unarmed, though. He swung down from his mule and grabbed the rifle Shifflet had dropped, along with jerking the man's Colt from its holster. Then he leaped back into the saddle and kicked the mule into motion.

Up ahead, Rostand had grabbed the reins of Jeanne's mule and was leading it toward the temple at a gallop while she hung on to the horn for dear life. Gullen was with them, swiveling in his saddle to throw lead at the Indians who were suddenly closing in from both sides of the boulevard. A couple more of Rostand's men fell, pierced by arrows.

Rostand, Jeanne, and Gullen reached the lane leading to the massive temple. They headed toward the pyramid with Captain Wood, the two Cubans, and the rest of the survivors thundering after them. Longarm brought up the rear, spraying bullets to hold back the furious mob following them.

There was an opening at the base of the pyramid, overhung by a sloping roof that continued down from the side of the structure itself. Thick pillars supported that roof. A couple of broad steps led into the temple. Rostand and the others rode the mules right up those steps and into a vast open space. Darkness was thick in there, but Longarm could tell the size by the way the hoofbeats echoed around.

He dropped out of the saddle and took cover behind one of the pillars. Several of the other men were doing the same thing, including Joshua Gullen and Rostand himself. Rifles cracked and lead scythed into the Indians who were coming up the flagstone path toward the temple. They sent a few more arrows toward the invaders, then dropped back, howling out their rage.

Gullen glanced over at Longarm as the shooting died away. "Maybe you were tellin' the truth about wantin' to throw in with us," he said.

"Or perhaps he's just trying to save his own skin," Rostand snapped. He pointed his rifle at Longarm. "Put the gun down, Marshal."

"You might want to think about that," Longarm drawled. "You lost several of your men out there, and there's a whole hell of a lot of angry Indians out there. I think it's gonna take every man we have to get out of here."

"He's right," Gullen said. "Who the hell figured there'd be a bunch of damn redskins squattin' here?"

Rostand cursed in French. "All right, all right. Distribute guns to all the men. That bunch of aborigines will attack again soon."

Longarm didn't know about that, and he regretted having to shoot the ones he had downed during the dash to the temple. They hadn't invited this bunch of loot-hungry varmints into their home, and you couldn't blame them for putting up a fight.

On the other hand, he wasn't going to stand by and let them kill him and his friends, either, regardless of the circumstances that had brought them here.

When everyone was armed, Rostand posted a man behind every pillar at the entrance to the temple, then said,

"Since we're here, I think we should go ahead and locate the treasure."

"You're worried about that now?" Jeanne asked. "When all of us may be on the verge of dying a horrible death?"

"I came here for the Treasure of the Sun," Rostand said stubbornly. "I mean to have it." He swung his rifle toward Gonzago. "I know you have been holding out the last bit of information I need, old man. Show me now, or I will—"

Gonzago stopped him with an upraised hand. "No need for threats, señor. I want to see the treasure myself. Have torches prepared, and we will find it."

The pitch-soaked torches that Rostand had brought along were quickly lit, and they cast their glare across the open space toward an arched doorway in the back. "Stay here," Rostand told Gullen.

"The hell with that," the gunman said. "I came all this way, too. I'm gonna have a look at that treasure for myself."

"I'm comin', too," Longarm said.

Rostand glared at him. "You seem to have forgotten that you are my prisoner, Marshal."

"I reckon we're past that now. We're all in this together."

After a moment, Rostand nodded curtly. "All right. Show us, old man."

Gonzago took one of the torches and led the way through the doorway into a large, stone-walled corridor. The walls had bizarre murals painted on them, and even though the primitive paint was faded, Longarm could make out enough to guess that the pictures represented ancient Aztec gods and rituals. Jeanne looked at them, too, and shuddered a little as she walked along close beside him.

There were five of them: Gonzago, Rostand, Jeanne, Gullen, and Longarm. Captain Wood had stayed in the front part of the temple to take charge of its defense if the Indians attacked again. Gonzago and Gullen carried torches. The shadows cast by the flickering flames made the long hall-way even more eerie.

They reached another open doorway. It led into a large, circular room. In the center of it was a stone altar of some sort. Longarm didn't doubt that human sacrifices had once been carried out on it. He glanced at the vaulted ceiling and saw a circular opening there, like a round chimney. At high noon, a column of light would shine down through that shaft, right onto the chest of the sacrificial victim whose still-beating heart was about to be carved out of his or her chest.

The torchlight showed lots of dark stains on the stone. Jeanne shuddered again.

Gonzago stepped to the altar, bent, moved a bit of stone that protruded from the side. For a moment, nothing happened.

Then, with a rumbling sound, the altar began to shift. It slid aside, revealing a narrow stone staircase that led down into darkness.

"The Treasure of the Sun," the old man murmured, "protected by the altar of the Sun God."

Chapter 24

Gonzago hesitated at the top of the stairs. Rostand snatched the torch out of his hand and said, "Give me that!" Holding the burning brand above his head, he started down.

Gullen motioned with his rifle at Longarm and Jeanne. "Go ahead," he ordered. "I ain't leavin' you up here, Long. You, too, old man."

Jeanne put a hand on the big lawman's arm. "Custis, I . . ."

"It'll be all right," he told her. "Come on."

He went down after Rostand, with Jeanne behind him, Gonzago following her, and Gullen bringing up the rear. When they reached the bottom, they found themselves in a chamber about twenty feet square.

The light bounced back dazzlingly from the gold and precious gems that filled the room.

Longarm had never seen anything like it. Gold jewelry, gold coins, massive bars of gold. Jewels in every color of the rainbow, glittering so brilliantly that they took the breath away and almost blinded the eyes. The legend was true. The Treasure of the Sun existed.

"Why didn't that old padre ever come back for it?" Gullen wondered aloud, his voice filled with awe.

"Because Fray Cristobal was a simple man," Gonzago

said. "He had no need for riches. He had his faith. As do I."

A rumble sounded from above. Gullen jerked his head toward the stairs. "What the hell!"

Gonzago moved faster than anyone would have thought an old man was capable of moving. He drove his aged body against Gullen, knocking the gunman off balance. Gonzago's gnarled hands snatched the revolver from Gullen's holster. He stepped back and leveled the gun at Gullen and Rostand.

"The altar is moving back into position," he said. "It stays open only a short time, and only the old high priests knew how to open it from down here. Marshal Long! Take the girl. Up the stairs! Now!"

Rostand took a step toward him. "You madman! We'll be trapped down here!"

"But you will have your treasure, señor," Gonzago said.

"Fuck that," Gullen said. He flung the torch in his left hand in Gonzago's face.

The old man pulled the trigger, but his involuntary flinching away from the flame threw off his aim. The bullet smacked into what looked like a solid gold chamber pot as the echoes of the shot slammed around in the room. The whipcrack of Rostand's rifle added to the din as he fired at Gonzago. The slug drove deep into the old man's belly and doubled him over.

The rifle in Longarm's hands blasted a split-second after Rostand's shot. The Frenchman cried out and staggered back as Longarm's bullet drilled his arm. He dropped the rifle.

"The hell with all of you!" Gullen yelled. "I'm gettin' out of here!"

He turned and lunged up the stone stairs.

Longarm shoved Jeanne after him. "Up you go!" he told her. "Get out of here!"

She hesitated for a heartbeat, then turned and fled as the rumbling became louder.

"Jeanne!" Rostand called after her as he clutched his bleeding arm. She didn't slow down.

Longarm covered Rostand and bent down to help Gonzago. "Come on, old-timer," he said.

Gonzago pushed Longarm's hand away and shook his head. "No, señor. I am dying, but what better place to leave this world than surrounded by the Treasure of the Sun?" A smile wreathed his wrinkled old face. "Please, my friend. Save yourself."

Another moment ticked past, then Longarm said, "*Vaya con Dios*, Gonzago." He began to back up the stairs, still covering Rostand. A glance over his shoulder showed him that Gullen and Jeanne had made it to the top of the staircase and out into the temple. The opening was now less than half the size it had been earlier, though, and the altar was still slowly closing across it.

Longarm turned and ran like hell, lunging up the steps two and three at a time.

Shots blasted below him. Rostand must have picked up his rifle with his left hand and was firing blindly after him. Slugs whined and bounced around him, but none of them found Longarm. He reached the top and flung himself through the hole in the floor, landing in a rolling sprawl.

Hearing footsteps slapping on the stairs, he turned to look back down the staircase and saw that Rostand was trying to escape. The Frenchman had dropped the rifle. Terror etched lines on his face as he realized how close he was to being trapped.

Then suddenly Gonzago appeared behind Rostand, throwing himself at the man's legs. The old man's arms caught Rostand around the knees and brought him down hard on the stairs. Rostand was almost at the top. He kicked and fought, trying to knock Gonzago loose while at the same time trying to reach up and pull himself to safety.

"You old fool!" he screamed. "They'll just work the lever and open the door again!"

Gonzago laughed, a wild pealing sound. "The alter moves only once, unless you know how to reset the mechanism!"

"No!" Rostand screeched. The opening was too narrow now for him to squeeze through it. Desperately, he thrust his arms through, then screamed again as the massive weight of the moving alter pinned them.

Longarm pushed himself back on the stone floor, grimacing as the altar rumbled into place once more. Rostand's arms, severed cleanly at the elbows, lay beside it as the blood leaked out of them and added to the dark stains already on the floor around the grim black stone.

"Custis . . ." Jeanne said.

Longarm hoped she hadn't seen that, but as he turned to look, he saw something even worse. Joshua Gullen had one arm wrapped around Jeanne's neck while the other hand held the muzzle of his Winchester at her throat.

"I reckon the Treasure of the Sun is all mine now," Gullen said.

Longarm laughed as he got to his feet. "Not hardly," he said. "Didn't you hear old Gonzago? You got to know the trick to make the altar move again, and we don't know it."

"I can figure it out, damn it. I can stay here as long as it takes once you're dead, Long."

"Have you forgotten about those Indians out there? You think they're gonna just let you stay here and study on it?"

"I don't know, but I do know I don't trust you. I'll figure it all out once you're dead. Now drop that rifle. I'd like to keep this gal alive, but I'll kill her if I have to."

Jeanne said, "Custis, no. Kill this dog. No matter what he does to me."

Longarm heaved a sigh. "I reckon he knows I can't let that happen." He bent to place the Winchester on the stone floor.

At that moment, Captain Wood yelled from the front of the temple, "Here they come again!"

Gullen's head turned, the rifle barrel dropped away from Jeanne's neck for a second, and she seized the chance to twist violently in his arms. She tore free from his grip and threw herself aside.

Longarm dived forward on his belly, scooping his rifle from the floor.

Gullen cursed and fired. The slug whipped through the

air above Longarm's head and ricocheted off the altar behind him. The Winchester in Longarm's hands roared as he sent a bullet smashing into Gullen's midsection. Gullen staggered back but managed to hang on to his rifle. Longarm worked the Winchester's lever and fired again. This time the bullet drove into Gullen's chest and knocked him off his feet. His rifle went clattering away across the stones.

As Longarm got to his feet and looked at Gullen's sprawled figure, he said, "That's for Mercedes, you son of a bitch."

He was vaguely aware that more rifles had been roaring while he and Gullen were trading shots, but the racket was dying away now. He grabbed Jeanne's arm and they ran toward the front of the temple to find out what was happening up there.

Valentine Wood met them. The captain's face was grimed with powder smoke, but he was grinning. "The devils turned tail and ran!" he said.

"You drove 'em off that easy?" Longarm asked, surprised.

Wood shook his head. "No, I think it was all the steam shootin' up from the ground that spooked 'em. Maybe they thought it was the spirits of all them dead Aztecs comin' back. To tell you the truth, I'm not so sure it ain't!"

Longarm took a deep breath. "I think we'd better make a run for it and get out of here."

"They may be layin' for us."

"If they are, we'll fight our way through. But I'll bet a hat they're gone. They'll be worried that we've disturbed the old gods, and if those hombres come back, they'll do it by blowin' the whole top off this mountain!"

They all mounted up as quickly as they could and burst out of the temple into the dusk. No arrows came flying toward them as they galloped up the boulevard toward the trail out of the caldera and the volcano crater. Longarm smelled brimstone in the air. The volcano might sit there for another five hundred years without erupting, or it might blow in the next five minutes. He just didn't know.

But he thought they ought to put as much distance between them and it as they could, just in case.

Trying to make it down the mountain trail in the dark was a hellish chore, but they made it without anybody falling off, thanks to the light from the torches that were still in the packs on the mules. By morning, they were at the bottom, and the volcano seemed to have settled back into its uneasy slumber behind them. Longarm let everybody rest for a while, but as soon as he thought they could make it, they set out across the valley for the pass that would take them out of the Devil's Range.

Jeanne was very quiet, which Longarm understood. Evil though he had been, Rostand was still her brother, and now he was lost to her forever. She had come all too close to losing her own life as well.

Late that afternoon, though, as she rode alongside Longarm, she said, "I suppose I am an even richer woman now. When we reach San Ramon, I will order the captain of the *Bellefleur* to take me home." She turned to look at the big lawman. "Will you come with me, Custis?"

He smiled. "Let's see . . . sleep on the cold ground and get shot at by outlaws as a deputy U.S. marshal, or live with a beautiful, rich, redheaded Frenchwoman?"

She laughed softly. "I have a feeling I know which one you will choose, Custis, mad though it may be."

"I reckon I'm too old and set in my ways to change now."

"A pity. But we can make the most of the time we have left together, no?"

"Yes," Longarm said.

Late that afternoon, they made camp in the pass. As Longarm and Jeanne stood looking back across the valley at the mountain, Captain Wood came over to them and said, "Look what I found in one of the packs."

In both hands, he held the Star of Father Cristobal.

Longarm took it, turned it over, gazed at the faint marks

scratched into the soft silver. They were gibberish to him, but they had led quite a few people to their destinies . . . and some of them would never come back.

"I wondered what had happened to it," he said. "I figured it was lost, along with the Treasure of the Sun."

"You will take it back to the mission in San Antonio?" Jeanne asked.

"That's the job my boss gave me. Knowin' Billy, he won't ask me too many questions about how I got it back . . . and I don't intend to tell him." He glanced toward the distant peak. "Some things are best left buried."

At that moment, a distant rumble sounded. Smoke and steam billowed up from the mountain's summit. A faint but definite vibration ran through the ground under their feet and then subsided, along with the rumbling sound. Evidently the sleeping giant wasn't quite ready to wake up just yet.

"The earth moved," Jeanne said.

"It sure did," Longarm agreed.

He intended to make it move again for the two of them, as many times as he could manage before they went their separate ways.

Watch for

LONGARM AND THE CROSS FIRE GIRL

the 391st novel in the exciting LONGARM
series from Jove

Coming in June!

GIANT-SIZED ADVENTURE FROM AVENGING ANGEL LONGARM.

BY TABOR EVANS

2006 Giant Edition:

LONGARM AND THE OUTLAW EMPRESS

2007 Giant Edition:

LONGARM AND THE GOLDEN EAGLE SHOOT-OUT

2008 Giant Edition:

LONGARM AND THE VALLEY OF SKULLS

2009 Giant Edition:

LONGARM AND THE LONE STAR TRACKDOWN

2010 Giant Edition:

LONGARM AND THE RAILROAD WAR

penguin.com/actionwesterns

M456AS0510

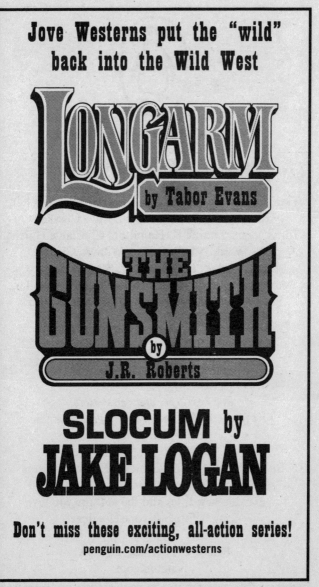

Jove Westerns put the "wild"
back into the Wild West

LONGARM
by Tabor Evans

THE GUNSMITH
by
J.R. Roberts

SLOCUM by
JAKE LOGAN

Don't miss these exciting, all-action series!

penguin.com/actionwesterns

M11G0610

Penguin Group (USA) Online

What will you be reading tomorrow?

Patricia Cornwell, Nora Roberts, Catherine Coulter,
Ken Follett, John Sandford, Clive Cussler,
Tom Clancy, Laurell K. Hamilton, Charlaine Harris,
J. R. Ward, W.E.B. Griffin, William Gibson,
Robin Cook, Brian Jacques, Stephen King,
Dean Koontz, Eric Jerome Dickey, Terry McMillan,
Sue Monk Kidd, Amy Tan, Jayne Ann Krentz,
Daniel Silva, Kate Jacobs...

You'll find them all at
penguin.com

*Read excerpts and newsletters,
find tour schedules and reading group guides,
and enter contests.*

Subscribe to Penguin Group (USA) newsletters
and get an exclusive inside look
at exciting new titles and the authors you love
long before everyone else does.

PENGUIN GROUP (USA)
penguin.com

M224G0909